Charles Stedman Ripley

The Ancestors of Lieutenant Thomas Tracy of Norwich,

Connecticut

Charles Stedman Ripley

The Ancestors of Lieutenant Thomas Tracy of Norwich, Connecticut

ISBN/EAN: 9783337724672

Printed in Europe, USA, Canada, Australia, Japan

Cover: Foto ©Raphael Reischuk / pixelio.de

More available books at **www.hansebooks.com**

TRACI : TRACYE : TRACY.

Or, an escallop, in the chief dexter
point, sable between two bendlets gules.
Crest On a chapeau gules, turned
up ermine, an escallop sable between
two wings expanded, or

THE

ANCESTORS OF LIEUTENANT THOMAS TRACY

OF

NORWICH, CONNECTICUT.

BY

LIEUTENANT
CHARLES STEDMAN RIPLEY.

United States Navy.

Member of the New-England Historic Genealogical Society.

AUTHOR OF "THE INGERSOLLS OF HAMPSHIRE," ETC.

———·——

BOSTON:
ALFRED MUDGE & SON, PRINTERS,
No. 24 FRANKLIN STREET.
1895.

To those Descendants

LIEUTENANT THOMAS TRACY

WHO HAVE AIDED, ENCOURAGED AND
ADVISED ME IN COLLECTING AND
COMPILING THE DATA OF
WHICH THIS BOOK IS
THE RESULT.

PREFACE.

After several years of correspondence, research and study, I now place in possession of my cousins all that I am able to ascertain from authentic records and writings, relative to the *historical lineage* of our common ancestor, LIEUTENANT THOMAS TRACY of Norwich, Connecticut.

The recent publication and indexing of many of the old British records has revealed much which hitherto has been hidden, and has aided very much in the compilation of the work. But the book is, nevertheless, incomplete, as many of the lines of descent have been lost in the mists of the past. The subject, however, has not been completely exhausted. In fact, this book is only a beginning. By diligently continuing the research, some other line, or lines, might, perhaps, be traced back to other distinguished historical characters, and other facts and incidents relating to the subject may be discovered.

From the following list of publications data relative to the Tracys has been obtained : —

Memoirs Illustrating the Noble Families of Tracy and Courtenay, Canterbury, 1796. History of Tewksbury, by James Bennett. Rudder's Gloucestershire. Bibliotheca Devoniensis, by James Davidson. Lipscombe's History of the County of Buckingham. Pedigrees of the Families of Tracy of Toddington, Sudeley of Sudeley, etc., etc. Historical and Descriptive Accounts of Toddington, Gloucestershire, by James Britton, F. S. A. Lodge's Peerage. Bank's Dormant and Extinct Baronage. Bank's Genealogical and Heraldic Gleamings, London, 1837. Burke's Extinct, Forfeited, and Dormant Baronetcies. Burke's Dormant, Forfeited, and Extinct Peerages of the British Empire. Burke's History of the Commoners. Burke's Peerage and Baronetage, 1886. Burke's Families of Royal Descent. The Roll of Battle Abbey, by the Duchess of Cleveland. The Writings of Sir William Dugdale. The Publications of the Harleian Society. Collectanea Topographica et Genealogica. The Index Library, issued by the British Record Society. Marshall's Genealogists' Guide. Caulkin's History of Norwich, Connecticut. Pedigree of the Tracy Family, 1843. The Historic Peerage of England, by Sir Harris Nicholas, G. C. M. G., London, 1857.

Trusting that in time another from among the descendants of our famous ancestors will continue the work which I have only begun, I send my manuscript to press.

CHARLES STEDMAN RIPLEY.

BOSTON, MASSACHUSETTS, 1895.

INDEX.

THE ANCESTORS OF LIEUTENANT THOMAS TRACY

OF

NORWICH, CONNECTICUT.

I.

THE ARMS OF TRACY

OF

BARNSTAPLE, DEVONSHIRE, AND STANWAY, GLOUCESTERSHIRE.

" Or, an escallop, in the dexter chief point, sable, between two bendlets gules."

CREST.

"On a chapeau gules, turned up ermine, an escallop sable, between
two wings, expanded, or."

No family in England can claim armorial bearings more
ancient than those of the Tracys. The heraldry of England dates from a period subsequent to the Norman
Conquest, and seems to have been introduced by William I.,
whose arms were "*Gules, two lions passant guardant, in
pale, or.*" These same arms were used by William II.,
Henry I., and Stephen.

The arms of Tracy were inherited by the brothers * Ralph
(*Lord de Sudeley*) and William (*Sir William de Traci*)
from their Norman ancestors, in about the middle of the
twelfth century. The emblazonry cannot be definitely

---

* See "The Norman Descent of Sir William de Traci," page 31.

traced back any further than this, but it was probably
derived from the shields of either the Sire de Traci or the
Count de Mantes. It is recorded that "Sir William de
Traci and his posterity differenced their coat amour from
the elder house of Sudeley by adding an *escallop shell* between the two bendlets." * The escallop shell, in those
days, when used as emblazonry, signified that the bearer, or
an ancestor who had had the same arms, had been beyond
the sea. This Sir William had done, having been to
Normandy.

At the beginning of the fourteenth century, during the
reign of Edward II., the arms of Tracy are referred to
(*VIII. Sir William Tracy, page* 36), and again in the
seventh year of the reign of Henry V. (*XIII. William
Tracy, page* 37).

In the official "Visitation of the County of Gloucester,
taken in the year 1623," † the arms of the Tracys of Stanway
were recorded as follows : —

"ARMS. Quarterly: 1 and 4, or, an escallop in the dexter chief point sable between two bendlets gules, *Tracye;*
2 and 3, argent, on a chevron sable between three pellets
as many roses of the field, *Baldington.*

"CREST. On a chapeau gules, turned up ermine, an
escallop sable, between two wings, expanded, or."

Thus we see, by referring to "The Tracy Line" (*page*
38), that Sir William Tracy, son of Henry Tracy, by his
wife Alice, daughter and co-heir of Thomas Baldington,
quartered the arms of his mother's family with those of his

---

* See Foot Note, " Sir William de Traci," page 35.

† At this time there were many persons in Gloucestershire who claimed
armorial bearings, to which they were not entitled. The arms of such
persons were defaced, and a list of their names may be found in the
records of the " Visitation."

father's. In this manner the arms were borne by his son, Richard Tracy of Stanway, and by his grandson, Sir Paul Tracy, Bart. The crest, as recorded during the "Visitation," is that of the Tracy family, and, as the chapeau indicates, is ancient in its origin.

The arms shown as the frontispiece are those of *Tracy*, and are displayed as those of an esquire, or gentleman, in accordance with the rules of heraldry.

The Tracy motto, "MEMORIA PII ÆTERNA"* (*the memory of the pious man is eternal*), is displayed below the arms, but its origin cannot be traced. No mention of it is made in the "Visitation" of 1623.

Coats-of-arms may be divided into three classes: First, those belonging to a man's European ancestors, and which have been used by them for many centuries. This is the most important class, and in most cases the original cause of the adoption of such arms is not to be discovered, and we must trust to the strictness with which this privilege was formerly guarded for a guarantee that the arms were justly appropriated. The second class embraces such arms as have been granted from the Herald's College, by royal command, as a reward for distinguished services rendered to the State. These instances are comparatively rare. The third class consists of the coats-of-arms granted by the Herald's College on payment of certain fees, and is rather a modern institution, though a few instances are recorded of a date prior to the settlement of New England. Arms of this latter class, though legal, can hardly be a source of much comfort to the possessor.

The "Arms of Tracy" are of the first-mentioned class, having been inherited by the early Tracys from their Nor-

---

* Fairbairn's Crests and Mottoes, Edinburgh, 1892.

man ancestors. Though some abuses have crept into the system, it is a fair assertion to make that coats-of-arms used prior to the seventeenth century were generally the rightful property of the users.

Crests are comparatively of modern origin. In the olden times they were used only by those who had won the right to them by personal services in some crusade. The Tracy Crest is ancient, and its form indicates that it originated in this manner. There are but few of similar kind and origin on record in England.

II.

LIEUTENANT THOMAS TRACY

OF

NORWICH, CONNECTICUT.

Thomas Tracy was a son of Sir Paul Tracy, Bart.. of Stanway, County of Gloucester, England. He was born in the year 1610 on the Tewksbury estates, probably at the manor of Stanway. He had scarcely reached his majority when people from all parts of England and from all classes of society, excepting the landed gentry, began to cross the Western Ocean in great numbers. In 1636, when the fever of emigration was at its height, and when men were emigrating who were in search of adventure and fortune, as well as those who were seeking a home in a new land, free from religious persecution and the oppression of an overbearing nobility, Thomas Tracy joined a band of emigrants and sailed for America. In this act he was probably influenced by the fact that he was a younger son in a very large family and without prospects of inheritance. In April of the same year he arrived at Salem, Massachusetts, where he resided until the following February, when he removed to Wethersfield, Connecticut. There he married, in 1641, Mary, the widow of Edward Mason, and then removed to Saybrook. Seven children were there born. About 1659 his wife died. He subsequently married two other wives, but had no issue by either. In 1645 he and Thomas Leffingwell, with others, relieved Uncas, the Sachem of Mohegan, with provisions when he was besieged at Shattuck's Point by Pessachus,

Sachem of the Narragansetts, which led to the subsequent grant of the town of Norwich in 1659. He and his family removed to Norwich in 1660, of which town he was one of the proprietors. In 1661 he was on a committee, appointed by the General Court, "to try the bounds of New London"; in 1662 he was chosen by the people one of the Court of Commission; in 1666 he was appointed ensign in the first Train Band of Norwich; in 1667, '70, '71, '72, '73, '75, '76, and '78 he was the deputy from Norwich to the Legislature, and in 1682, '83, and '85 from Preston. He sat as a member of the Colonial Assembly at more than twenty sessions. In 1673 he was commissioned lieutenant of the New London County Dragoons, raised to fight the Dutch and Indians. In 1678 he was appointed a justice. He died at Norwich. November 7, 1685,* in the seventy-sixth year of his age.

"Thomas Tracy was well educated for the time in which he lived. This placed him to advantage among the leading men of the colony directly upon his arrival. Throughout a long life, the Legislature frequently appointed him upon important committees, and he held his full share of public offices, legislative, military, and magisterial. He was a gentleman of consequence in the community, a thorough business man, and of the very best personal character." (*Robinson.*)

His children by his first wife were —

JOHN,	born	1642.
THOMAS,	"	1644.
JONATHAN,	"	1646.
MIRIAM,	"	1648.
SOLOMAN,	"	1651.
DANIEL,	"	1652.
SAMUEL,	"	1654.

---

* Records of the Town of Norwich, Connecticut.

All of these children married and had families, except Daniel, who died Jan. 11, 1693, *sine prole*.

NOTE. — Lieutenant Thomas Tracy's second wife, married at Norwich about 1678, was Martha Bourne, daughter of Thomas Bourne, of Marshfield, Massachusetts, and widow of John Bradford. His third wife, married at Norwich, 1683, was Mary Foote, daughter of Nathaniel and Elizabeth (Deming) Foote of Wethersfield, and widow of John Stoddard, who died in 1664, and then of John Goodrich, who died in 1680.

III.

THE PARENTS OF LIEUTENANT THOMAS TRACY.

Lieutenant Thomas Tracy died in Norwich, Connecticut, November 7, 1685, in the seventy-sixth year of his age, therefore he was born between the dates November 7, 1609, and November 7, 1610 (*old style*). He was born in Gloucestershire, in the vicinity of Tewksbury, and was a grandson of Richard Tracy of Stanway. Of this we are very certain, for his immediate descendants write these facts, the information having been obtained from Thomas himself. It is also probable that Thomas stated who his father was; but the name seems to have been forgotten, or carelessly omitted. In the early days of the American Colonies people were not very particular in keeping their family records. It is also possible that the name of his father was intentionally suppressed, as the feeling among the colonists at that period was very bitter against the aristocracy and the system of hereditary rights, and a son of an English baronet naturally would have been somewhat reticent relative to his birth. In a "Pedigree of the Tracy Family," written in 1843 "by one of his descendants," he is spoken of as "*a descendant of Richard Tracy of Stanway*," but the name of his father is not mentioned. Later comes the "Hyde Genealogy," and in this Lieutenant Thomas Tracy is made *the son of Nathaniel Tracy, a son of Richard Tracy of Stanway.* In "Browning's Americans of Royal Descent," which follows, Lieutenant Thomas Tracy of Norwich is *a son of Nathaniel Tracy of Tewksbury and a grandson of Richard Tracy of Stanway.* "Burke" gives the three sons of Richard Tracy of Stanway as follows: (1) *Paul*, the eldest, heir and successor of his father; (2) *Nathaniel;* (3) *Samuel.* It has always been supposed, from the early writings of the American Tracys, that Thomas was a younger son of a younger son of Richard Tracy of Stanway; and, as Samuel resided in Herefordshire after his marriage, he could not have been his son and have been born in Gloucestershire. Reasoning thus, and knowing that Nathaniel resided in Gloucestershire, from the fact that he was the sheriff of that county in the year 1586, Nathaniel became the father of Thomas.

During the "Visitation of the County of Gloucester," which occurred in 1623, a genealogical chart of the family was made out. In this Richard and his children are given as follows : —

RICHARD TRACY of Stanway,══BARBARA, dau. of Thomas Lucy,
Gloucestershire, | of Charlecote, Warwickshire.

HESTER.	NATHANIEL.	SUSAN.	JUDITH.	PAUL.	SAMUEL,
m.		m.	m.	m.	of Clifford,
Roland Smarte.		1. Edward	Francis Throg-	1. Anne, dau. of	Co. Hereford.
		Barker of	morton.	Raffe Shark-	m.
		Rogester.		erley, Co.	Catherine, dau.
		2. Sir Henry		Northampton,	of Thomas
		Bellingsley,		by Alice, dau.	Smythe of
		Knt., and		of Hugh Rad-	Campden.
		Alderman		cliff.	
		of London.		2. Anne, dau. of	
				Sir Ambrose	
				Nicholas, Knt,	
				Lord Mayor	
				of London.	

The above chart is probably correct, and no better authority can be obtained, as Paul, then living and the head of the house, undoubtedly knew the names of his brothers and sisters, the order of their births, and the names of those whom they married.

If Nathaniel was the eldest son, he died *sine prole,* previous to 1623, as, otherwise, Paul could not have succeeded to the Manor of Stanway.

Whether the eldest or a younger son, Nathaniel, in order to have been the father of Thomas, should have been married previous to 1610, and had he married at any time previous to 1623, Paul certainly would have known it, and so have stated in his genealogical chart. The estate of Stanway was a part of the confiscated lands of Tewksbury, formerly belonging to the Abbey of Tewksbury (*see page* 41), and to suppose that Nathaniel married and became the father of a family, residing in the near vicinity of the manor, and that this fact should not be mentioned in the records of the "Visitation" of 1623, nor any allusion made to his children (*then or in after years*), while the records of his youngest brother's family, residents of another county, were made up complete at Stanway, as were also those of his sisters, is impossible.

At the time of the "Visitation" the dates of births, marriages, and deaths were not filled in on this chart, and this accounts for there being no further data relative to Nathaniel.

The following is the genealogical chart of the family of Samuel, youngest child of Richard Tracy of Stanway : —

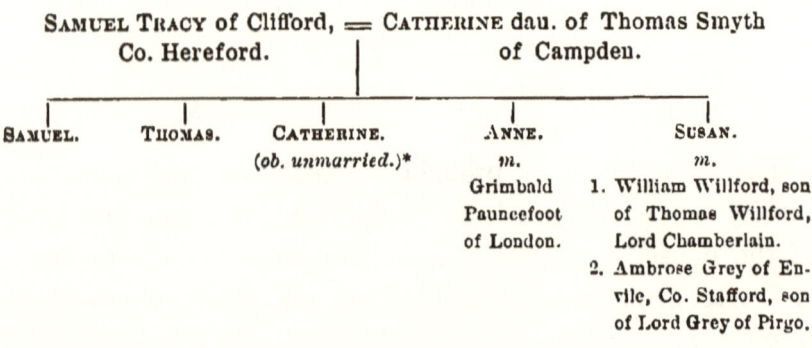

SAMUEL TRACY of Clifford, = CATHERINE dau. of Thomas Smyth
    Co. Hereford.   of Campden.

SAMUEL.	THOMAS.	CATHERINE.	ANNE.	SUSAN.
		(*ob. unmarried.*)*	*m.*	*m.*
			Grimbald	1. William Willford, son
			Pauncefoot	of Thomas Willford,
			of London.	Lord Chamberlain.
				2. Ambrose Grey of En-
				vile, Co. Stafford, son
				of Lord Grey of Pirgo.

* Not originally on the chart.

From the above we see that the second son of Samuel, the youngest son of Richard, was named Thomas, but this Thomas was born in Herefordshire — not in Gloucestershire — and previous to the year 1601. (*Records of the Herald's College.*)

Passing now to the family of Sir Paul Tracy, Bart., son of Richard Tracy of Stanway, we find that he was the father of twenty-one children by his first wife, and that this wife died in 1615. (*Records of Gloucestershire in the Herald's College.*) By his second wife there was no issue. Therefore, all his children were born previous to 1616. One of the youngest children, Thomas (*see page* 43), was born in 1610 and baptized in 1611. (*Records in possession of the Herald's College.*)

Thus, of the *two* grandsons of Richard Tracy of Stanway whose names were *Thomas*, there can be but little doubt which one was Lieutenant Thomas Tracy of Norwich, Connecticut.

In the chancel of Bansted Church, Surrey, is a white marble slab on which is cut the following inscription : —

> Here under lieth the corpse of Paule Tracy, who
> Died the 1st day of June 1618, sonne of Paule
> Tracy, esquier, and Margaret his wife, sonne of
> Sir Paule Tracy of Stanway in the county of
> Gloucester, Baronet, and Margaret, the daughter
> of Philip Moss, esquier, of Cannon in the
> County of Surrey. 1619.

Upon the first reading of this inscription it would seem that *Margaret*, the daughter of Philip Moss, was the *wife* of Sir Paul Tracy, and consequently the *mother* of Lieutenant Thomas Tracy, as there were no children by the second wife. Lodge, in his "Peerage of Ireland," reads the inscription in

this way. This reading, however, *is incorrect*. The real
meaning of the wording is that the "corpse" was a son of
Paul Tracy, Esquire, and *Margaret, his wife*. It is then
further stated that Paul Tracy, Esquire, was a son of Sir
Paul Tracy of Stanway, and that *Margaret, his wife (wife
of Paul Tracy, Esquire)*, was a daughter of Philip Moss.
The year 1619 is the date of cutting and placing the slab.
By carefully reading the inscription it will become quite
plain that the name "*Margaret*," which appears twice, is
intended for *one and the same person*.

In the records of the Herald's College it is distinctly
stated that "*Anne Sharkerley*" was the first wife of Sir
Paul Tracy of Stanway, and that "*Margaret*," daughter of
"*Phillip Moyse*" of Bansted, County of Surrey, was the
first wife of Paul Tracy, Esquire. This corresponds with
the statement of Sir Paul Tracy, who declares that "*Anne,
dau. of Raff Sharkerley, Co. Northampton, by Alice, dau.
of Hugh Radcliff*," was his first wife.

From the evidence presented it seems to be proven that
Thomas was a younger son of Sir Paul Tracy of Stanway
by his wife, Anne Sharkerley.

IV.

VIKINGS, BRITONS, AND WEST SAXONS.

ANCIENT ANCESTORS OF CERDIC, FIRST KING OF THE WEST SAXONS.
OF ECGBERHT, FIRST KING OF ENGLAND, AND OF SIR WILLIAM
DE TRACI, KNIGHT OF GLOUCESTERSHIRE.

I.   **WODEN,** whom some antiquarians claim to have descended from the eldest son of the patriarch, Noah, made himself master of a considerable part of the north of Europe in the third century, and died in what is now Sweden.   By his wife, FREA, or FRIGGA, he had six sons* : —

> WECTA.
> CASER.
> WETHELGEAT.
> WELDEG.
> BELDEG.
> EAXNETA.

II.   **BELDEG,** sometimes called **BALDER,** the fifth son, married NANNA, a daughter of GEWAR, and had a son —

III.   **BRANDIUS,** or **BRANDO,** who was father of —

IV.   **FROODIGARIUS,** or **FROETHGAR,** who had a son—

V.   **WIGGA,** who was the father of —

VI.   **GEWESIUS,** or **GEWISCH,** whose son —

VII.   **EFFA,** or **ESTA,** was father of —

VIII.   **EFFA** (*the second*), whose son —

IX.   **ELISEUS,** was the father of —

X.   **CERDIC,** the first King of the West Saxons.

NOTE. — Flountius, a monk of Worcester, writing in the first quarter of the twelfth century, shows that Cerdic descended from Woden, as above.   Woden is sometimes called *Odin,* and was called by the Romans *Othinus.*

* Speed's History of England.

V.

THE WEST SAXON LINE.

ANCESTORS OF ECGBERHT OF ENGLAND AND OF SIR WILLIAM
DE TRACI.

I.   **CERDIC,** the first King of the West Saxons, died in 534, after having reigned about thirty-three years. He had two sons, Kenric, his successor, and Chelwulf, who died during the lifetime of his father, and whose great-grandson, Kentwin, was the seventh King of the West Saxons.

II.   **KENRIC** succeeded to the crown in 534, upon the death of his father. He died in 560, having reigned twenty-six years. He was succeeded by his eldest son, Cheaulin. His second son, Cuthwulf, died in 572, leaving a son, Cearlik, who wrested the kingdom from Cheaulin, his uncle, in 592, and was fourth King of the West Saxons.

III.   **CHEAULIN** succeeded to the crown upon the death of his father in 560, and reigned about thirty-two years, when he was dethroned by his nephew and banished from the kingdom. He died in exile in 593, leaving two sons, Cuthwin and Cuth.

IV.   **CUTHWIN,** his eldest son, was killed in battle with the Britons in 584, during the reign of his father. He left two sons, Kenwald and Cuth.

V.   **CUTH** died, leaving a son —

VI.   **CHELWALD,** who was the father of Kenred.

VII. **KENRED** had four sons and one daughter. His eldest son, Iua, was the eleventh King of the West Saxons. Another of his sons was —

VIII. **INGILLS,** who was the father of —

IX. **EOPPA,** who left a son —

X. **EASA,** who was the father of —

XI. **ALKMUND,** or **ÆTHELMUND,** whose son, Ecgberht, became the seventeenth King of the West Saxons and the first King of England.

VI.

THE DESCENT OF SIR WILLIAM DE TRACI

FROM THE SAXON KINGS OF ENGLAND.

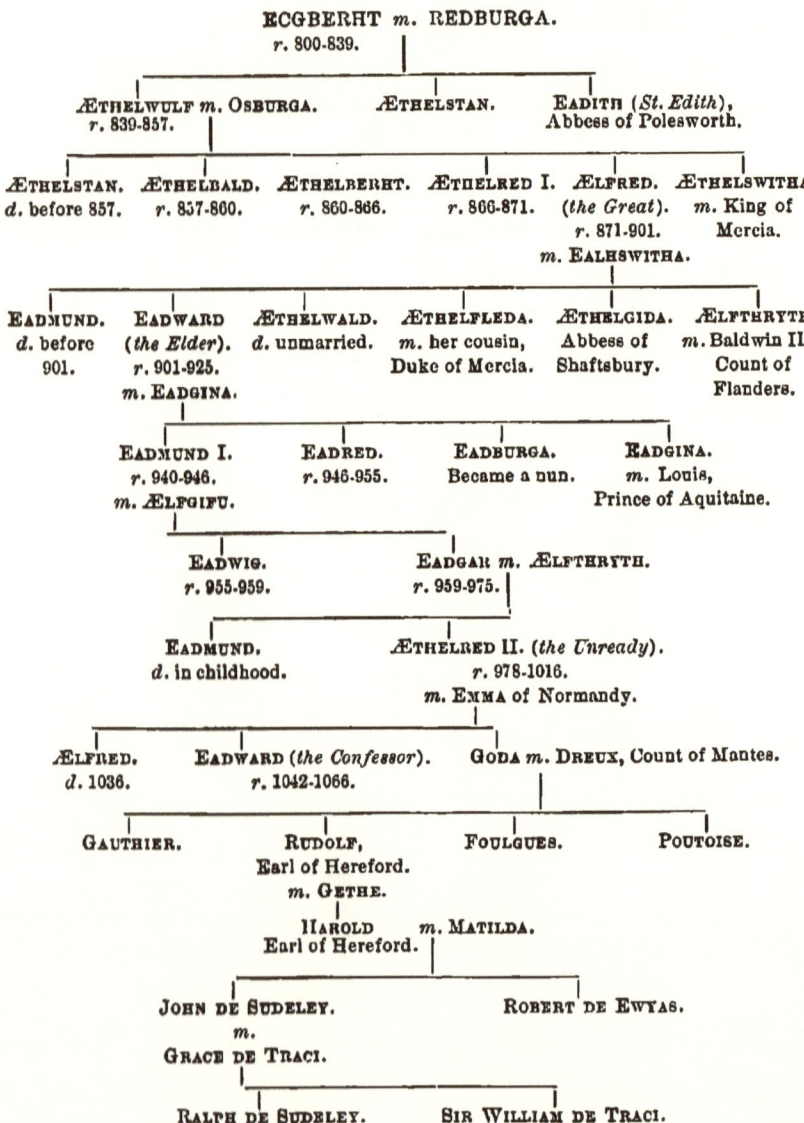

ECGBERHT *m.* REDBURGA.
r. 800-839.

ÆTHELWULF *m.* OSBURGA.   ÆTHELSTAN.   EADITH (*St. Edith*),
r. 839-857.   Abbess of Polesworth.

ÆTHELSTAN. ÆTHELBALD. ÆTHELBERHT. ÆTHELRED I. ÆLFRED. ÆTHELSWITHA.
d. before 857. *r.* 857-860. *r.* 860-866. *r.* 866-871. (*the Great*). *m.* King of
                                                                                r. 871-901.   Mercia.
                                                                        m. EALHSWITHA.

EADMUND. EADWARD ÆTHELWALD. ÆTHELFLEDA. ÆTHELGIDA. ÆLFTHRYTH.
d. before (*the Elder*). *d.* unmarried. *m.* her cousin, Abbess of *m.* Baldwin II.,
901.   *r.* 901-925.   Duke of Mercia. Shaftsbury. Count of
        m. EADGINA.   Flanders.

EADMUND I.   EADRED.   EADBURGA.   EADGINA.
r. 940-946.   *r.* 946-955.   Became a nun.   *m.* Louis,
m. ÆLFGIFU.   Prince of Aquitaine.

EADWIG.   EADGAR *m.* ÆLFTHRYTH.
r. 955-959.   *r.* 959-975.

EADMUND.   ÆTHELRED II. (*the Unready*).
d. in childhood.   *r.* 978-1016.
                              m. EMMA of Normandy.

ÆLFRED.   EADWARD (*the Confessor*).   GODA *m.* DREUX, Count of Mantes.
d. 1036.   *r.* 1042-1066.

GAUTHIER.   RUDOLF,   FOULGUES.   POUTOISE.
              Earl of Hereford.
              m. GETHE.

              HAROLD   *m.* MATILDA.
              Earl of Hereford.

JOHN DE SUDELEY.   ROBERT DE EWYAS.
      m.
GRACE DE TRACI.

RALPH DE SUDELEY.   SIR WILLIAM DE TRACI.

I. **ECGBERHT,** the son of Æthelmund, sometimes called Alkmund, succeeded to the West Saxon crown upon the death of King Bithrick, in the year 800, and in the course of the first twenty years of his reign he succeeded in uniting the whole heptarchy under his rule. He was the seventeenth king of the West Saxons and the first Saxon king of all England. He married the LADY REDBURGA, and by her had two sons and one daughter.

II. **ÆTHELWULF,** his eldest son and successor, took for his wife, OSBURGA, a daughter of OSLAC, an English nobleman and a direct descendant of Cerdic, and by her he had five sons and one daughter. After the death of Osburga, in his old age, he married a young wife, Judith, a daughter of Charles the Bald, Emperor and King of France, and great-granddaughter of the Emperor Charlemagne. He died Jan. 18, 857, without issue by her. She subsequently married Baldwin, the first Count of Flanders. She was ancestress of Matilda, the wife of William the Conqueror.

III. **ÆLFRED THE GREAT,*** born in 849, was the youngest son of Æthelwulf. He survived all his brothers

---

* " Alfred was fond of visiting and informing himself of the condition of every class of his subjects. On one occasion he set out, accompanied by a courtier named Ethelbert, and in his rambles stopped at the house of Albanac, a chieftain of rank and power, whose name would indicate his descent to have been rather British than Saxon. This nobleman received his sovereign with welcome, and his wife and three daughters, all of whom were extremely beautiful, attended on him, as was the custom. The dignified deportment of Elswitha, one of the young Saxon ladies, and the grace and elegance of her person, eclipsed that of her sisters at supper, when waiting upon the King. Alfred was much attracted with her charms, and praised her beauty in glowing terms. The impression made upon him was observed by Albanac, who, when the company separated for the night, communicated his suspicions to his

and became the sixth King of England when about twenty-one years of age.   In 869 he married EALSWITHA, a daughter of the Earl of Lincolnshire, and by her he had three sons and three daughters.   He died Oct. 28, 901, and Ealswitha died about 904.

IV. **EADWARD THE ELDER,** second son of Ælfred the Great, succeeded his father.   He was married three times, and it was from the third wife that Sir William de Traci was descended.   This third wife, EADGINA, was a daughter of Earl Sigeline, and by her he had two sons and two daughters.   She survived her husband nearly forty years, dying Aug. 25, 963.

wife. The King, on his part, at retiring. had confided to Ethelbert his admiration of Elswitha, who, with a courtier's tact, approved of his choice. Next morning, when day broke, Albanac presented himself at the door of his royal guest, requesting immediate admittance. The King bade him enter; on which, to his surprise, he beheld Albanac, with a drawn sword in his hand, conducting his three daughters, who, clad in the deepest mourning, seemed overwhelmed with the most poignant distress. 'What is it I see?' exclaimed Alfred. 'A father,' returned Albanac, 'whose honor is more dear to him than life itself. You are my King and I am your subject, but not your slave. You are well acquainted with my illustrious ancestors, and it is now proper you should know my sentiments. Last night you discovered a particular attraction in my daughter. If you have conceived the idea of dishonoring my house you see the sword that shall in an instant sacrifice these unhappy victims, willing to sacrifice themselves; but if a pure flame is kindled in your breast, my alliance will not disgrace the crown: choose, therefore, and name her that is born to such distinguished honor!'

"This somewhat abrupt proceeding, the legend goes on to say, did not displease Alfred, who, appreciating the noble and daring courage of the father of Elswitha, immediately professed his readiness to make her his wife, and she was soon afterwards Queen. That the King had chosen his partner wisely, was proved by subsequent events. Elswitha was virtuous and amiable, and inspired her noble husband with a lasting affection for her." (*Lives of the Queens of England before the Norman Conquest. —Hall.*)

V. **EADMUND I.**, eldest son of Eadward the Elder by his third wife, succeeded his half brother, King Æthelstan, and reigned until he was assassinated, May 26, 946. In the first year of his reign (940) he married Ælfgifu (*the fairies' gift*), and had by her two sons. He was succeeded by his brother Eadred, who reigned until 955.

VI. **EADGAR**, the second son of Eadmund I., born in 943, succeeded to the crown in 959. He married in 961 Æthelflæda the Fair, daughter of Earl Ordmar. By her he had one son, Eadward, born about 962, who succeeded him in 975, and afterwards became known as Eadward the Martyr. For a second wife he married (964) Ælfthryth, a daughter of Ordgar, Duke of Devonshire, and widow of Earl Æthelwold, and by her had two sons :—

Eadmund, born in 965 and died in childhood.

Æthelred, born in 967, and succeeded his half brother, Edward the Martyr.

Note. The first wife of Edward the Elder was Ecguina, the daughter of a shepherd, and by her he had two sons and one daughter.

Æthelstan, his successor, reigned 925-940.

Ælfred, died during the lifetime of his father.

Eadith, married Selrick, the Danish King of Northumberland, and afterwards became the Abbess of Tamworth and was known as "Sister Beatrice."

The second wife was Ealfleda, a daughter of Earl Æthelhelme, and by her he had two sons and six daughters.

Ealsward, died about 925.

Eadwin, drowned during reign of his half brother, Æthelstan.

Ealfleda, Abbess of Ramsey.

Ecguina, became the second wife of Charles III. of France.

Æthelhild, became a nun.

Eadhild, married Hugh the Great, Duke of France and Burgundy and Count of Paris and Orleans, father of Hugh-Capet.

Eadgitha, married Otho the Great, Emperor of Germany.

Ealgina, married a nobleman of Italy.

Otho the Great had another wife, Adelheida, of Burgundy, who was the mother of Adélaide. See page 50.

VII. **ÆTHELRED II.,** called "The Unready," succeeded to the crown in 978, upon the assassination of his half brother, Eadward the Martyr. He married, when about seventeen years of age, Ealfleda, daughter of the Erldorman Thored. His second wife was Emma of Normandy,* the youngest daughter of Richard the Fearless, third Duke of Normandy. By his wife, Queen Emma, he had two sons and one daughter : —

> Ælfred, whose eyes were put out by order of Harold Harefoot, and who died in the monastery where he was imprisoned.
>
> Eadward (*the Confessor*), who succeeded his half brother, Harthacnut, as King of England.
>
> Goda, who married the Count of Vixin.

Æthelred II. died April 23, 1016, and after his death Emma married Cnut of England and Denmark.

VIII. **THE PRINCESS GODA,** daughter of Æthelred II., by his wife Emma of Normandy, held lands in Gloucestershire in the reign of her brother, Eadward the Confessor,† which lands remain in possession of some of her descend-

---

Note. — Children of Æthelred II., by his first wife, Ealfleda : —

> Æthelstan, died about 1011.
>
> Ecgberht, died young and unmarried.
>
> Eadmund (*Ironsides*), who succeeded his father and reigned April 23—Nov. 30, 1016.
>
> Eadred, died when about 22 years of age.
>
> Eadwig, who survived all his brothers of the full blood, and was murdered at the instigation of Cnut the Dane in 1017.
>
> Eadgar, died in childhood.
>
> Eadgitha married Eadrick, the Duke of Mercia.
>
> Ealfgina, married Utred the Bold.
>
> (*Daughter*), married an English nobleman.

* Ancestry of Emma of Normandy, see "The Norman Dukes," pages 97–100.

† See 2 Ellis' Doomsday, 119.

ants at this time. She married for her first husband DREUX,* Count of Mantes. He went on a pilgrimage to Jerusalem, and died in Bithynia about the first of July, 1035. They had four sons. For a second husband she married Eustace of Boulogne. She died in 1054. By her first husband, the Count of Mantes, she had four sons : —

> GAUTHIER, who is sometimes called WALTER.
> RUDOLF, (*Rudolph* or *Ralph*).
> FOULGUES.
> POUTOISE.

IX. **RUDOLF DE MANTES**, the second son of the Count of Mantes by his wife, the Princess Goda, was lord of the Manor of Sudeley and of Toddington, which he inherited from his mother. He was created Earl of Hereford by his uncle, Eadward the Confessor, of which earldom his son was deprived in the reign of William the Conqueror. In the year 1051 he was admiral of fifty ships of the king's navy. He married GETHE, who held lands in her own right in Buckinghamshire, and who in Doomsday Book is called " *Gethe, wife of Earl Rudolph.*" He died Dec. 21, 1057, and was buried at Peterborough.

X. **HAROLD DE MANTES**, Earl of Hereford, and only son of Rudolf de Mantes and his wife, Gethe, married MATILDA, daughter of HUGH-LUPUS,† the Earl of Ches-

---

* Dreux, who was Count of Vixin, in France, is called by English historians Walter de Mantes, Count of Mantes. He was a great-grandson of Waleran, who succeeded Hugh the Great, Duke of France, as Count of Vixin, in 956.

† Hugh, surnamed " Lupus," was a Norman nobleman and a nephew of William the Conqueror. He was a son of Richard-goz, Viscount d'Auveranche, and his wife Margaret, a half sister of William. In 1070 his uncle gave him the Earldom of Chester, which, since 1066, had been held by Georbodus, a Fleming. He married Ermentrude, the daughter of Hugh de Clermont, and had a daughter, Matilda. See page 31.

ter, and ERMENTRUDE, his wife, and by her had two sons
John de Sudeley and Robert de Ewyas.

XI. **JOHN DE SUDELEY,** the eldest son, inherited the
lands of his father in Gloucestershire and became Lord of
Sudeley and Toddington. He married GRACE DE TRACI,
daughter and heiress of HENRI DE TRACI, feudal Lord
of Barnstaple in Devonshire. There were two sons born :
RALPH, the heir of the father, and WILLIAM, who inherited
the lands of his mother and assumed her family name of
DE TRACI, becoming, as a knight of Gloucestershire,
SIR WILLIAM DE TRACI.

VII.

THE NORMAN DESCENT OF SIR WILLIAM DE TRACI,

ANCESTOR OF LIEUTENANT THOMAS TRACY OF NORWICH, CONNECTICUT.

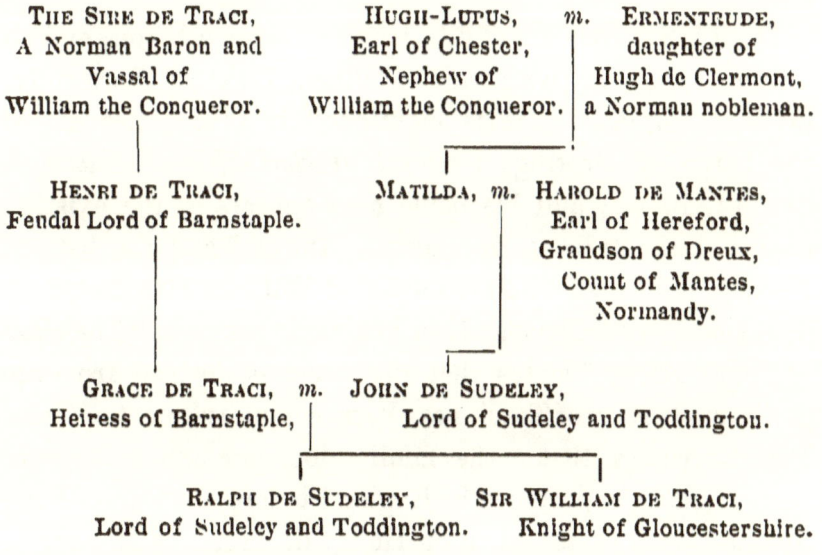

| THE SIRE DE TRACI, A Norman Baron and Vassal of William the Conqueror. | HUGH-LUPUS, Earl of Chester, Nephew of William the Conqueror. | *m.* ERMENTRUDE, daughter of Hugh de Clermont, a Norman nobleman. |

HENRI DE TRACI, Fendal Lord of Barnstaple.

MATILDA, *m.* HAROLD DE MANTES, Earl of Hereford, Grandson of Dreux, Count of Mantes, Normandy.

GRACE DE TRACI, *m.* JOHN DE SUDELEY, Heiress of Barnstaple, Lord of Sudeley and Toddington.

RALPH DE SUDELEY, Lord of Sudeley and Toddington.

SIR WILLIAM DE TRACI, Knight of Gloucestershire.

NOTE. Although surnames, as personal soubriquets, were known in England from a very early period, hereditary surnames seem not to have been in use until after the Norman Conquest, and not in general use until the beginning of the fifteenth century. During the eleventh, twelfth, and thirteenth centuries surnames were taken up in a very gradual manner by the descendants of both Saxons and Normans. By the middle of the twelfth century families of rank considered a surname a necessary appendage to distinguish them from those of meaner extraction. In France and Normandy it was customary for the eldest sons to take their fathers' surnames or the names of their fathers' estates, while the younger sons assumed the names of the estates allotted to them. This plan seems to have been introduced into England by the Normans, and there prevailed for some time.

VIII.

THE TRACY LINE.

THROUGH GRACE DE TRACI, DAUGHTER AND HEIRESS OF HENRI DE TRACI, FEUDAL LORD OF BARNSTAPLE IN DEVONSHIRE.

I. **THE SIRE DE TRACI** was a Norman baron, and an officer in the army with which William, Duke of Normandy, invaded England. He is mentioned in Wace's account of the battle of Hastings (*fought at Senlac, near Hastings, Oct.* 14, 1066); and his name also appears on the existing copies of the "ROLL OF BATTEL ABBEY," and the lists of Norman noblemen who accompanied William into England. The Duchess of Cleveland, in her work entitled, "*The Roll of Battle Abbey*," states that the name is derived from the castle and barony of Traci, near Vire, Arrondissement of Caen. Planché writes that "the family does not appear to have been of much importance in England before the time of King Stephen, who bestowed upon Henry de Traci the Honour of Barnstaple in Devonshire; but the first of the name we hear of is Turgis, or Turgisius, de Traci, who, with William de la Ferté, was defeated and driven out of Maine by Fulk de Rechin, Count of Anjou, in 1073, and who was, therefore, in all probability, the Sire de Traci in the army of Hastings."

NOTE. — The "Roll of Battel Abbey." By order of William, a monastery was erected on the very spot where he had gained that decisive victory which gave him the crown of England, from which circumstance it was called "Battel Abbey." The names of those who had fought with him were inscribed on a roll and placed in the abbey.

II. **HENRI DE TRACI,**[*] a son of the Sire de Traci, seems to have settled in the County of Devon, and was the only man of noble birth in that county who stood firm to the king during the invasion of the Empress Maud, and, as he was an "excellent soldier," he rendered considerable service "in those western parts." As a recognition of his loyalty, King Stephen gave him the "Honour and Barony of Barnstaple," which formerly had been enjoyed by Iahel, the son of Alured de Torneis. He died about 1146, leaving a daughter, Grace, who inherited his possessions.

III. **GRACE DE TRACI,**[†] daughter and heiress of Henri de Traci, lord of Barnstaple, married, about 1130, JOHN DE SUDELEY, lord of Sudeley and Toddington, and son of Harold de Mantes, Earl of Hereford, and had issue : —

> RALPH DE SUDELEY, the heir and successor of his father, and founder of the Priory of Erdburic.
>
> WILLIAM DE TRACI, who inherited from his mother, and assumed her family name.

IV. **SIR WILLIAM DE TRACI,** the second son, lived in the reign of Henry II., and held lands of his brother, Ralph de Sudeley, by one knight's fee. This holding was the Manor of Toddington, for it appears by "Domesday Book" that it was held by the Lord Sudeley, of the Manor of Sudeley, and, in the reign of Edward I., the Tracys are expressly said to be possessed of it; and this William, in a

---

[*] The Historic Peerage of England, by Sir Harris Nicholas, G. C. M. G., London, 1857. Burke's Peerage and Baronetage, 1886. In the work of Sir Harris Nicolas, the descendants of this Henri de Traci are incorrectly given, but in Burke's work of 1886 the correct descent will be found under "Sudeley."

[†] Some authorities state that Grace was an only child, and that the male line became extinct upon the death of Lord Henri.

deed of Otwell, Lord of Sudeley, son and heir of the said Ralph, is called his uncle. Sir William was one of the four knights who, in 1170, at the instigation of King Henry II., assassinated Thomas à Becket, Archbishop of Canterbury. Fuller, in his "*Worthies of England*," names the assassin as "*Sir William Tracy, of Toddington*," and describes him as "*a man of high birth, state and stomach, a favorite of the king's, and his daily attendant.*" In the nineteenth year of the reign of Henry II. (1171), he was created "Justiciary" of Normandy, and we know that for a time he performed the duties of that office, for he was present at Falaise in 1174, when William, King of Scotland, did homage to Henry II., and in 1176 he was succeeded in his office by the Bishop of Winchester. Subsequently, Sir William returned to England. During the reign of King John he appeared in arms against his sovereign with the other rebellious barons, and in consequence his lands were confiscated by the crown. At the beginning of the reign of Henry III., however, these lands were restored to him, as is shown by a roll, dated at Westminster, Nov. 18, second year of the reign of Henry III. (1218). During the latter part of his life he seems to have repented of the murder of the archbishop, for he founded and endowed a chapel to *Thomas à Becket*, in the Conventual Church at Tewkesbury.

"There exists a generally received tradition," writes the Duchess of Cleveland, "that he retired to his estates in the West of England, where 'he lived a private life, when the wind and weather turned against him'; and according to the local history of his native County of Gloucester, reached the good old age of ninety. His residence was at Morthoe, close to Woollacomb Bay, and the worthy folks of Devonshire aver that his tormented spirit may, even now, be heard moaning and lamenting on the Woollacomb sands, where it is doomed to wander restlessly to and fro, toiling to 'make bundles of sand and wisps of the same' for all time to come. He was, it is said, buried at Morthoe, where an effigy, by some believed to be his, remains in the church."

Sir William de Traci died at Morthoe, County of Devon, in 1224. By HAWISE DE BORN, his wife, he left a son and heir and two daughters.

V. SIR HENRY DE TRACY of Toddington, County of Gloucester, his eldest son and heir, died about the year 1246, leaving a daughter and two sons : —

> MARGERY, wife of Maurice de Stanliuch.
> HENRY, his heir.
> THOMAS, who became, "*jure uxoris Isoldae de Cardinan*," of Restormel Castle, Cornwall.

VI. SIR HENRY DE TRACY of Toddington appears in a charter, July 26, 1260, and was summoned to perform military service at Carmarthen, in the eleventh year of the

---

NOTE. — " Sir William de Traci and his posterity differenced their coat armour from the elder house of Sudeley by adding an escallop shell between the two bendlets." (*Herald's College.*)

NOTE. — Woollacomb-Tracy, Bovey-Tracy, Nymet-Tracy, Newton-Tracy, and Bradford-Tracy, in Devonshire, still bear Sir William's surname.

NOTE. — The Oliver de Tracy who was living in 1184, and who, in the older editions of " Burke," is given as the son of Sir William, and whom Sir Harris Nicholas makes a son of Sir Henry, was a son of Sir Gervase Courtenay. This Sir Gervase Courtenay married one of the daughters of Sir William de Traci, and one of his sons, Oliver, assumed the family name of his mother.

NOTE. — It will be observed that the surname of Sir Henry, son of Sir William, is written " *de Tracy*," instead of " *de Traci*," the change having been made by him. His grandson, Sir William, omitted the " *de*." Some writers spell the name " *Tracey*." It has also been written " *Tracye*."

reign of Edward I. He died in 1296, and was succeeded by his son. His children were —

> WILLIAM, his son and heir.
> EVE, wife of Guy de Bryan.

VII. **SIR WILLIAM TRACY** of Toddington, who is recorded among the knights of Gloucestershire in the seventeenth year of the reign of Edward I. (1288), and with Ralph de Sudeley, his kinsman, is stated to have had a command in the Scottish war. He left a son and heir, —

VIII. **SIR WILLIAM TRACY** of Toddington, who was in ward to Laurence Tresham in the twenty-ninth year of the reign of Edward I. (1300). At the beginning of the reign of Edward II. (1307) he was at the tournament at Dunstable, as appears by an old drawing of a knight in armour, bearing a standard, upon which are the arms of the family. In the seventeenth year of the same reign he was appointed, jointly with John Bermansel, High Sheriff of Gloucestershire, which office in those times was of great importance and authority. He was twice elected to Parliament as one of the kinghts of Gloucestershire. In a roll of the nobles of England, dated at Berwick, June 30, 1315, appears the name of William Tracy. Sir William left a daughter and a son and heir : —

> MARGERY, wife of John Archer, of Umberslade.
> WILLIAM, his heir.

IX. **WILLIAM TRACY**, Esquire, of Toddington. In the seventh year of the reign of Edward III. (1333), a mandate was issued to this William Tracy and to Thomas Berkeley of Coberle, to raise three hundred men from the forest of Dene and two hundred men in the County of Gloucester. He died leaving a son and heir, —

X. **SIR JOHN TRACY** of Toddington, Knight of Gloucestershire, thirty-second year of the reign of Edward III. (1358). For five years in succession, commencing in 1358, he was sheriff of the county. He died in 1363, leaving three children : —

> John, his heir and successor.
> Margaret, wife of Sir Thomas de Langley, Knt.
> Dorothy,* wife of Edmond Bray, of Barrington, in Gloucestershire.

XI. **SIR JOHN TRACY** of Toddington, Member of Parliament and sheriff for Gloucestershire. He died in 1379, leaving two children : —

> William, his heir and successor.
> Margaret, wife of Robert Fitz-Elys.

XII. **WILLIAM TRACY,** Esquire, of Toddington, was the High Sheriff of Gloucestershire in 1395. He died in 1399, leaving a son and heir, —

XIII. **WILLIAM TRACY,** Esquire, of Toddington, was called to the Privy Council of Henry IV., as appears by a private letter, still extant, written by the king in the most flattering terms, and dated 21 July, 1401, *"from my manor of Sutton."* In the fifth year of the reign of Henry V. (1417), he was appointed the High Sheriff of Gloucestershire. Two years later (7th Henry V.), being "one of those persons of quality in the county of Gloucester who bearing ancient arms from his ancestors, and holding by tenure," he had summons "to serve the king in person for defense of the relm."

---

* In the Tracy Records the name of Sir John's third child is not given, but in the records of the Brays of Barrington she is named, and it is stated that she was a daughter of Sir John Tracy of Toddington.

He married ALICE, the widow of William Gifford, and the eldest daughter and co-heiress of SIR GUY DE LA SPINE,* Knt., Lord of Coughton, County of Warwick, and had issue : —

WILLIAM, his heir and successor.
JOHN.
ALICE, wife of Hugh Culme, of Moland, Devon.

XIV. WILLIAM TRACY, Esquire, of Toddington, was the Sheriff of Gloucestershire during the twenty-second and twenty-third years of the reign of Henry VI. He married MARGERY, a daughter of SIR JOHN PAUNCEFORT,† Knt., by his wife, a daughter of SIR ANDREW HERLE. He died in 1460, leaving two sons and a daughter : —

HENRY, his heir.
RICHARD.
MARGERY, wife of Thomas Mylle, Esq., of Horscombe, County of Salop.

XV. HENRY TRACY, Esquire, of Toddington, the eldest son, married ALICE, daughter and co-heir of THOMAS BALDINGTON, Esquire, of Alderley, County of Oxford. He died about 1506, leaving issue : —

WILLIAM, his heir.
RICHARD, who married and had issue.
RALPH, "A monke and prior of the Charterhowse by Syon and was there slayne by Goodwyn a monke of the same howse."
ANNE, who married, (1) William Wye; (2) Thomas Mannington.
ELIZABETH, who married, (1) ——— Langley; (2) Sir Alexander Baynham.

XVI. SIR WILLIAM TRACY, of Toddington, the eldest son, was the Sheriff of Gloucestershire during the fifth year of the reign of Henry VIII. (1513). "He was a gentleman of excellent parts and sound learning, and

---

* See page 45.
† See " The Pauncefort Line," page 44.

is memorable for being one of the first who embraced the reformed religion in England, as appears by his last will, dated 22 Henry VIII. (1530)." After his decease, this will was condemned in the Bishop of London's Court, and an order sent to Parker, Chancellor of Worcester, to raise his body (1532). But the chancellor too officiously burned the corpse, the recorder only warranting him to raise the body according to the law of the church. In consequence he was afterwards fined £400 and turned out of the chancellorship. Sir William married Margaret, a daughter of Sir Thomas Throckmorton, of Cross Court, in Gloucestershire. He died about 1531, leaving issue : —

> William,* his heir, who married Agnes, a daughter of Simon Digbye.
>
> Robert, who died *sine prole.*
>
> Richard, who received from his father the Manor of Stanway.
>
> Alice, who married ——— Owgan.

Sir William's famous will is a curious document, — most characteristic of the times, — and the first portion of it reads as follows : —

"In the Name of God Amen."

I, WILLIAM TRACY, of Toddington, in the County of Gloucester, make my Testament and last Will, as hereafter followeth :

First and before all things I commit my self to God, and to his Mercy, believing, without any doubt or Mistrust, that by his Grace, and the Merits of Jesus Christ, and by the virtue of his Passion and Resurrection, I have, and shall have, Remission of all my Sins, and Resurrection of Body and Soul, according as it is written :

---

* William was ancestor of Viscount Tracy of Rathcoole, in the peerage of Ireland, and of Robert Tracy, who was one of the English judges from 1700 to 1726.

"*I believe that my Redeemer liveth, and that at the last day I shall rise out of the Earth, and in my Flesh shall see my Saviour.*" This my hope is laid up in my bosom.

And touching the Wealth of my Soul, the faith that I have taken and rehearsed, is sufficient, as I suppose, without any other Man's Works or Merits. My Ground and Belief that there is but one God, and one Mediator between God and Man, which is JESUS CHRIST; so that I accept none other in Heaven or in Earth to be Mediator between me and God, but only JESUS CHRIST; all others to be but as Petitioners in receiving of Grace, but none able to give Influence of Grace; and therefore will I bestow no part of my goods for that Intent, that any man shall say or do to help my soul, for therein I trust only to the promises of Christ, "*He that believeth, and is baptized, shall be saved, and he that believeth not, shall be damned.*"

As touching the burying of my body, it availeth me not whatsoever be done thereto; for St. Augustine saith, *De Cura agenda pro Mortuis*, that the Funeral Pomps are rather the Solace of them that live, than the Wealth and Comfort of them that are dead, and therefore I remit it only to the discretion of my Executors.

And touching the distribution of my temporal Goods, my purpose is, by the Grace of God, to bestow them to be accepted as the Fruits of Faith; so that I do not suppose that my Merit shall be by the Good bestowing of them, but my Merit is the Faith of JESUS CHRIST only, by whom such Works are good; according to the words of our Lord: "*I was hungry and thou gavest me Meat, &c.*" And it followeth, "*That which ye have done to the least of my Brethren; ye have done it to me:*" and ever we should consider the true saying, "That a good Work maketh not a good man, but a good man maketh a good work; for Faith maketh a man both good and righteous, for a righteous man liveth by Faith, and whatsoever springeth not of Faith, is Sin."

For my Temporal Goods . . .

NOTE. — The passages from Scripture which appear in Sir William Tracy's will were probably quoted from memory.

XVII. **RICHARD TRACY,** Esquire, of Stanway, the third son, obtained from his father the Manor of Stanway, in the County of Gloucester, part of the lands of the Abbey of Tewksbury, which came into the family by grant from the crown. " This Richard," says an old writer, " was well educated, and wrote learnedly of his father's faith several treatises in the English tongue, and the most remarkable one, entitled '*Preparations to the Cross*,' written experiment- ally, having suffered much in his estate for his father's reputed heretical will : he also wrote prophetically, 1550 (a few years before the beginning of Queen Mary's reign), another treatise, ' *To Teach One to Die,*' which, with his '*Preparations to the Cross,*' which was reprinted, and falsely ascribed by the editor to be composed by John Frith, being one of the three that was found in the belly of a cod brought into the market to be sold at Cambridge, A. D. 1626, wrapped about with canvas, very probably what that voracious fish plundered out of the pocket of some ship- wrecked seaman." In the second year of the reign of Queen Elizabeth (1560), Richard Tracy was the Sheriff of Gloucestershire. He married BARBARA LUCY, a pupil of Fox, the martyrologist, and daughter of SIR THOMAS LUCY,* Knt., of Charlecote, in Warwickshire. By her he had three sons and three daughters. He died in 1569. (*Records of Gloucestershire.*)

HESTER, who married " Roland Smarte."

NATHANIEL, who was Sheriff of Gloucestershire about 1586, and who probably died *sine prole* previous to 1623.

SUSAN, who married, first, " Edward Barker of Rogester," and, sec- ond, " Sir Henry Billingsley, Knt., and Alderman of London,"

JUDITH, who married " Francis Throgmorton."

PAUL, who succeeded to the Manor of Stanway.

SAMUEL, of Clifford, Herefordshire, and who married Catherine, a daughter of " Thomas Smythe of Campden."

---

* See " XVII. Sir Thomas Lucy, Knt.," page 67.

XVIII. **SIR PAUL TRACY,** Bart., eventually came into possession of the Manor of Stanway. He was created a baronet, June 29, 1611, by King James I., "being the thirteenth created from the institution of the order. He married, first, ANNE, daughter and heiress of RAFFE (*Ralph*) SHARKERLEY, of Ayno-on-the-Hill, County of Northampton, by ALICE, daughter and heiress of HUGH RADCLIFF. This wife died in 1615. (*Records of Gloucestershire.*) His second wife was Anna, daughter and heiress of Sir Ambrose Nicholas, Knt., Lord Mayor of London. This wife died in 1625. (*Parish Register.*) By his first wife twenty-one children were born, but by his second wife there was no issue. Sir Paul died in 1626 (*Records of Gloucestershire*), and was succeeded by his eldest son.

His children by his first wife were : —

> RICHARD, born about 1587; married, about 1610, Anne, daughter of Sir Thomas Coningsby of Hampton, County of Hereford, and was the heir and successor to his father. His eldest son, Humphrey, was born in 1612, according to the official records in the Herald's College, but the family record says "1616." He had two other sons, Richard and John. Each of his sons succeeded to the title in turn. All died *sine prole.*
>
> ELIZABETH, wife of Gyles Carter of Sewell, County of Gloucester.
>
> HESTER, wife of Francis Kerle of Much-Marcle, County of Hereford.
>
> PAUL, of "Pickadille Hall, nigh James Court," County of Middlesex, married, first, Margaret, daughter of Phillip Moyse of Bansted, County of Surrey; second, Mary, daughter of George Limiter of Canterbury, in Kent.
>
> SUSAN, died unmarried.
>
> BARBARA, wife of Richard Smith of the Middle Temple.
>
> SUSANNA, died unmarried.
>
> ALEXANDER.
>
> ALICE.
>
> LUCY, born about 1603; wife of Bray Ayleworth, County of Gloucester.
>
> MARGARET, died unmarried.

SHARKERLEY, died *sine prole.*

SUSAN (2), born about 1606; married to William Price of Winchester, one of the grooms of the King's Privy Chamber. She died March 13, 1632, "before she had been married full 14 weeks."

SAUNDERS.

NATHANIEL, died in infancy.

WILLIAM, died *sine prole.*

NATHANIEL (2).

THOMAS, born in 1610; emigrated to America in 1636. (*Town Records of Salem, Mass.*)

JOHN, died *sine prole.*

VICESSIMUS, so named because he was the twentieth child.

ANNE, wife of Edward Halle of Henwick, in the County of Worcester; and after his death, married William Ingraham of Erlescourt, in the County of Worcester.

NOTE. — There is no certainty that the twenty-one children of Sir Paul Tracy, Bart., are all given in the order of their birth. Thomas, however, was the ninth son, and, in 1623, was the seventh living son.

IX.

THE PAUNCEFORT LINE.

FROM "THE VISITATION OF THE COUNTY OF GLOUCESTER, TAKEN IN THE YEAR 1623."

ARMS: Gu. 3 lions ramp. arg.

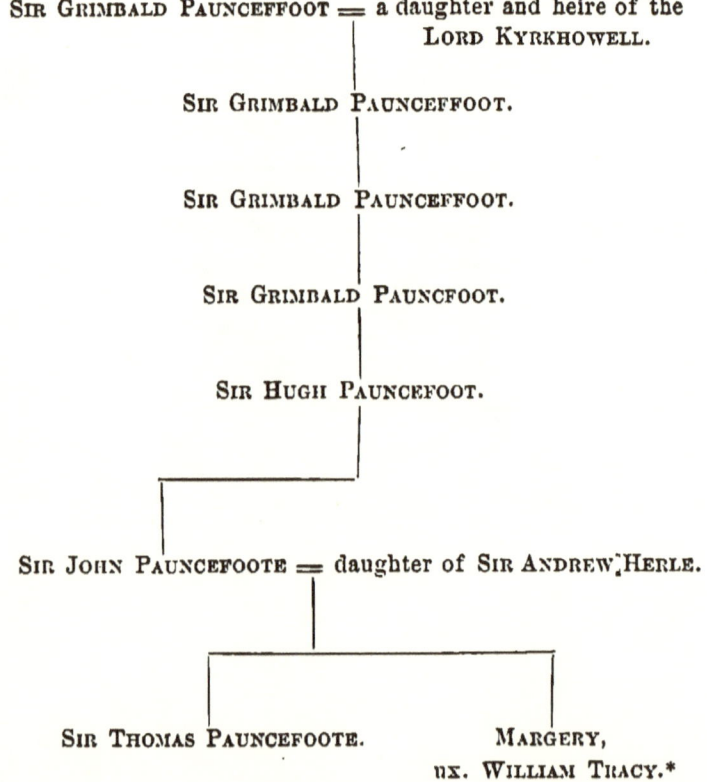

SIR GRIMBALD PAUNCEFFOOT ═ a daughter and heire of the
LORD KYRKHOWELL.

SIR GRIMBALD PAUNCEFFOOT.

SIR GRIMBALD PAUNCEFFOOT.

SIR GRIMBALD PAUNCFOOT.

SIR HUGH PAUNCEFOOT.

SIR JOHN PAUNCEFOOTE ═ daughter of SIR ANDREW HERLE.

SIR THOMAS PAUNCEFOOTE.   MARGERY,
                             ux. WILLIAM TRACY.*

---

* See "XIV. William Tracy, Esquire," page 38.

X.

THE TRACY MARRIAGES.

SHOWING THE DESCENT FROM THE TWO SISTERS, ALICE AND
ELEANOR, THE CO-HEIRESSES OF COUGHTON.

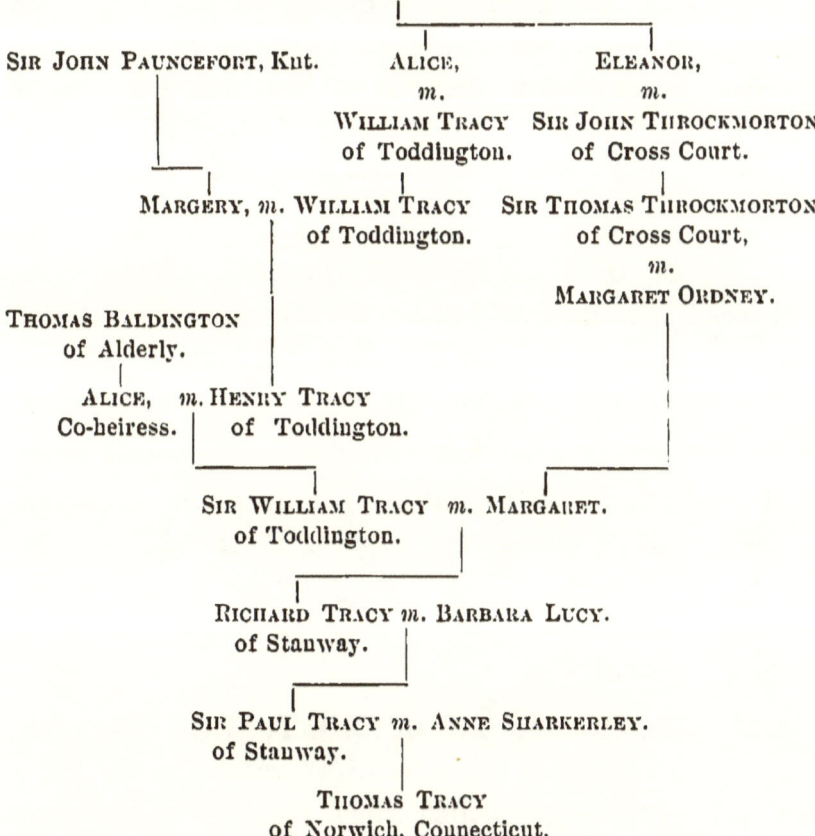

SIR GUY DE LA SPINE,
Lord of the Manor of Coughton.

SIR JOHN PAUNCEFORT, Knt.   ALICE,   ELEANOR,
                              m.   *m.*
                      WILLIAM TRACY   SIR JOHN THROCKMORTON
                      of Toddington.   of Cross Court.

MARGERY, *m.* WILLIAM TRACY   SIR THOMAS THROCKMORTON
              of Toddington.   of Cross Court,
                                  m.
                              MARGARET ORDNEY.

THOMAS BALDINGTON
of Alderly.

ALICE,   *m.* HENRY TRACY
Co-heiress.   of Toddington.

SIR WILLIAM TRACY   *m.* MARGARET.
of Toddington.

RICHARD TRACY *m.* BARBARA LUCY.
of Stanway.

SIR PAUL TRACY *m.* ANNE SHARKERLEY.
of Stanway.

THOMAS TRACY
of Norwich, Connecticut.

SIR GUY DE LA SPINE. " He was knight for Warwickshire in the
Parliaments of King Richard II., and Escheator of that county and of
Leicestershire; whose father, William, held notable employments in the
former county, in the reign of Edward III., and was grandson to William
de la Spine, who married Johanna, daughter and co-heir to Sir Simon de
Cocton (*now called Coughton*), the lineal heir male to Ralph, son of William de Cocton; who were all persons of great account, and flourished at
that place before the reign of Henry II." (*Lodge.*)

XI.

THE THROCKMORTONS.

ANCESTORS OF MARGARET THROCKMORTON, WIFE OF SIR WILLIAM TRACY OF TODDINGTON.

THROCKEMERTONIA, THROCKMORTON, or the ROCKMOOR TOWN, from which the family of THROCKMORTON obtained its name, is situated in the vale of Evesham, in the Parish of Fladbury, anciently written *Flandenburgh*, County of Worcester, and was a manor containing two hamlets, Hull (*Hill*) and Moor.

I. **JOHN OF THROCKMORTON** was in possession of and was the lord of said manor in 1130, and it is believed that the family possessed it before the Norman invasion. The etymology of the name is British, or Saxon. From this John we pass to his descendant,—

II. **JOHN THROCKMORTON**, Lord of Throckmorton, in the thirteenth year of the reign of Edward III. (1339). He had in marriage AGNES,* daughter and heiress of SIR RICHARD ABBERBURY, of Abberbury, in the County of Oxford, and had issue.

III. **SIR THOMAS THROCKMORTON**, the eldest son, was of the retinue of the Earl of Warwick, in the twentieth year of the reign of Richard II. (1396) was Escheator of Worcestershire in the third year of the reign of Henry IV., and in the sixth year of the same reign he was Constable of Elmley Castle. He married AGNES BESFORD, an heiress, and left a son and heir.

---

* This Agnes, wife of John Throckmorton, and daughter of Sir Richard Abberbury, is sometimes called "Anne."

IV. **SIR JOHN THROCKMORTON** was a man of some prominence during the reigns of Henry V. and Henry VI. During the latter reign he was the Under Treasurer of England. His will is dated at "*London*, 12 *April*, 23 *Henry VI*." He bequeathed his body to be buried in the parish church of St. John the Baptist, at Fladbury, requesting that his executors should provide a marble stone of such largeness as might cover as well the graves of his father and mother as his own, and that of his wife in case she should determine to repose there. He died in the same year, as appears by the probate, leaving ELEANOR, his wife, surviving. She was the daughter and co-heiress of SIR GUY DE LA SPINE, Lord of Coughton, in Warwickshire. By this lady he had three sons and five daughters.

V. **SIR THOMAS THROCKMORTON,** his eldest son and heir, married MARGARET ORDNEY, and had issue. One of their daughters, MARGARET, married SIR WILLIAM TRACY, of Toddington. (*Burke's Extinct, Forfeited, and Dormant Baronetcies.*)

NOTE.—In June, 1682, Sir William Throckmorton, ninth in descent from Sir Thomas Throckmorton and his wife, Margaret Ordney, fell in a duel, and the title became extinct.

XII.

THE DESCENT OF THE PRINCESS GUNDRED,

DAUGHTER OF WILLIAM THE CONQUEROR AND MATILDA OF FLAN-
DERS, AND ANCESTRESS OF BARBARA LUCY, WIFE OF RICHARD
TRACY OF STANWAY.

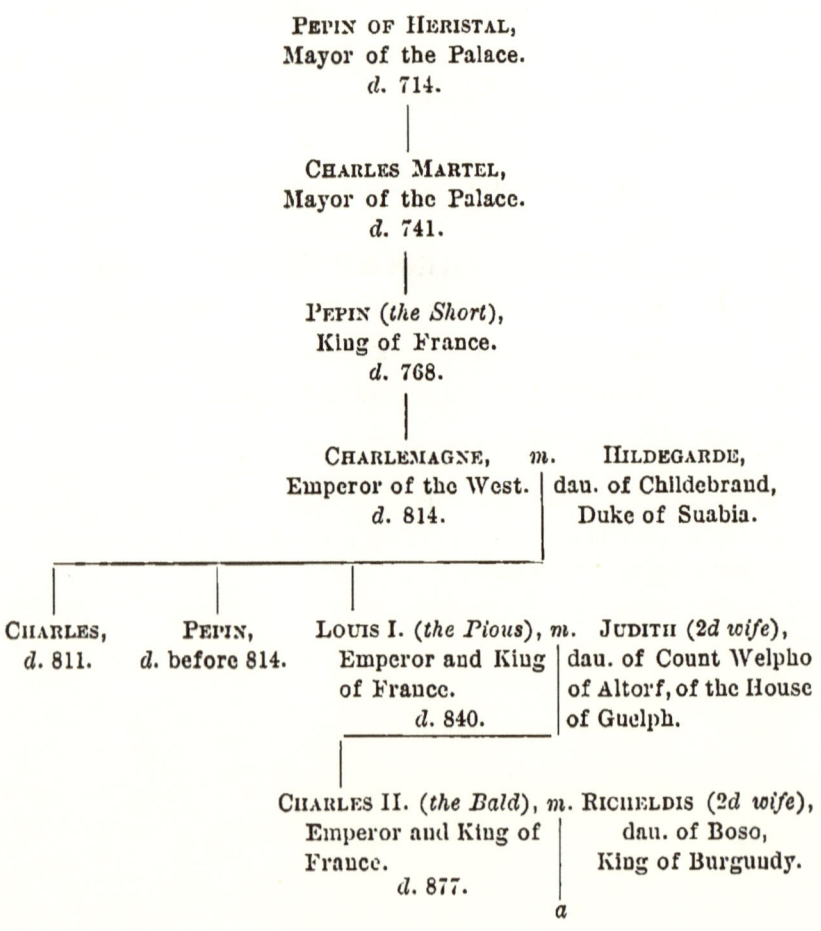

PEPIN OF HERISTAL,
Mayor of the Palace.
d. 714.

CHARLES MARTEL,
Mayor of the Palace.
d. 741.

PEPIN (*the Short*),
King of France.
d. 768.

CHARLEMAGNE,   *m.*   HILDEGARDE,
Emperor of the West.   dau. of Childebrand,
d. 814.   Duke of Suabia.

CHARLES,   PEPIN,   LOUIS I. (*the Pious*), *m.*   JUDITH (*2d wife*),
d. 811.   *d.* before 814.   Emperor and King   dau. of Count Welpho
of France.   of Altorf, of the House
d. 840.   of Guelph.

CHARLES II. (*the Bald*), *m.* RICHELDIS (*2d wife*),
Emperor and King of   dau. of Boso,
France.   King of Burgundy.
d. 877.
a

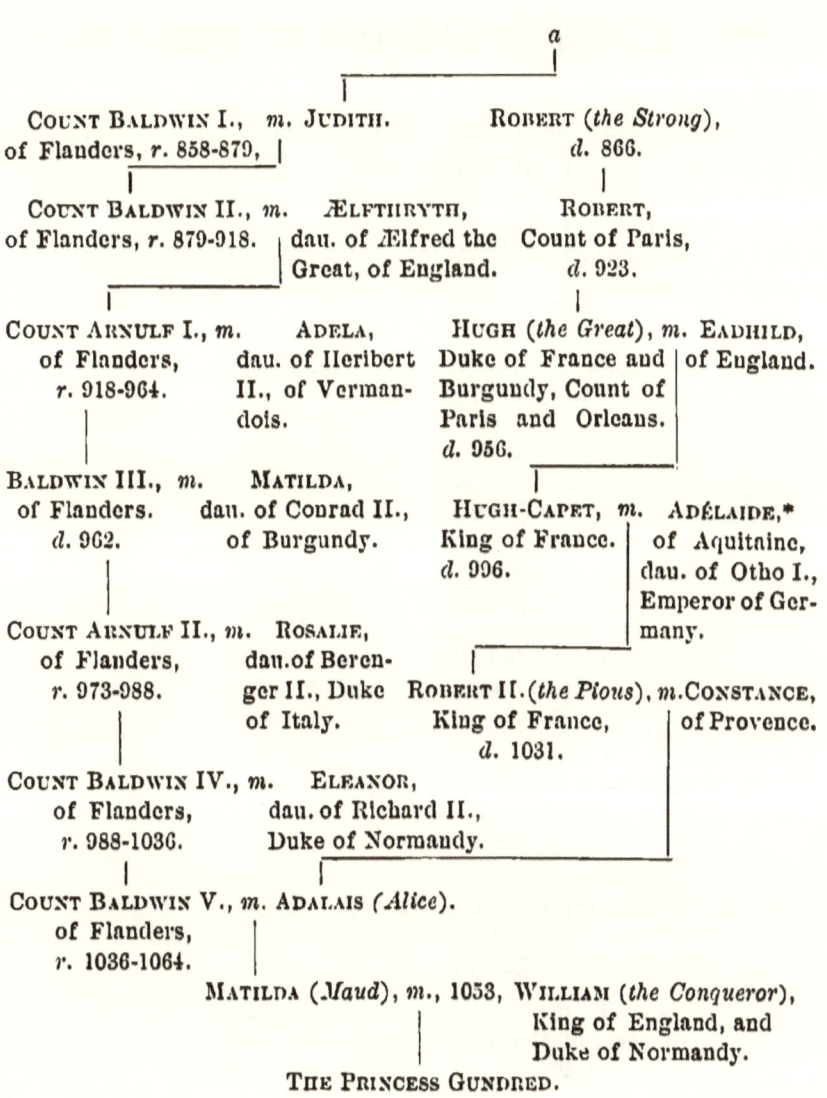

a

COUNT BALDWIN I., *m.* JUDITH.   ROBERT (*the Strong*),
of Flanders, *r.* 858-879,   *d.* 866.

COUNT BALDWIN II., *m.*   ÆLFTHRYTH,   ROBERT,
of Flanders, *r.* 879-918.   dau. of Ælfred the   Count of Paris,
                              Great, of England.   *d.* 923.

COUNT ARNULF I., *m.*   ADELA,   HUGH (*the Great*), *m.* EADHILD,
   of Flanders,   dau. of Heribert Duke of France and   of England.
   r. 918-964.   II., of Verman-   Burgundy, Count of
                       dois.   Paris and Orleans.
                                         d. 956.

BALDWIN III., *m.*   MATILDA,
of Flanders.   dau. of Conrad II.,   HUGH-CAPET, *m.*   ADÉLAIDE,*
   d. 962.   of Burgundy.   King of France.   of Aquitaine,
                                          d. 996.   dau. of Otho I.,
                                                              Emperor of Ger-
COUNT ARNULF II., *m.*   ROSALIE,   many.
   of Flanders,   dau.of Beren-
   r. 973-988.   ger II., Duke   ROBERT II.(*the Pious*), *m.*CONSTANCE,
                      of Italy.   King of France,   of Provence.
                                         d. 1031.
COUNT BALDWIN IV., *m.*   ELEANOR,
   of Flanders,   dau. of Richard II.,
   r. 988-1036.   Duke of Normandy.

COUNT BALDWIN V., *m.* ADALAIS (*Alice*).
   of Flanders,
   r. 1036-1064.

          MATILDA (*Maud*), *m.*, 1053, WILLIAM (*the Conqueror*),
                                        King of England, and
                                        Duke of Normandy.
          THE PRINCESS GUNDRED.

* Ancestry of Adélaide of Aquitaine. See page 50.

XIII.

THE DESCENT OF ADÉLAIDE OF AQUITAINE,

Wife of Hugh-Capet, King of France, and Ancestress of the Princess Gundred and Barbara Lucy, wife of Richard Tracy of Stanway.

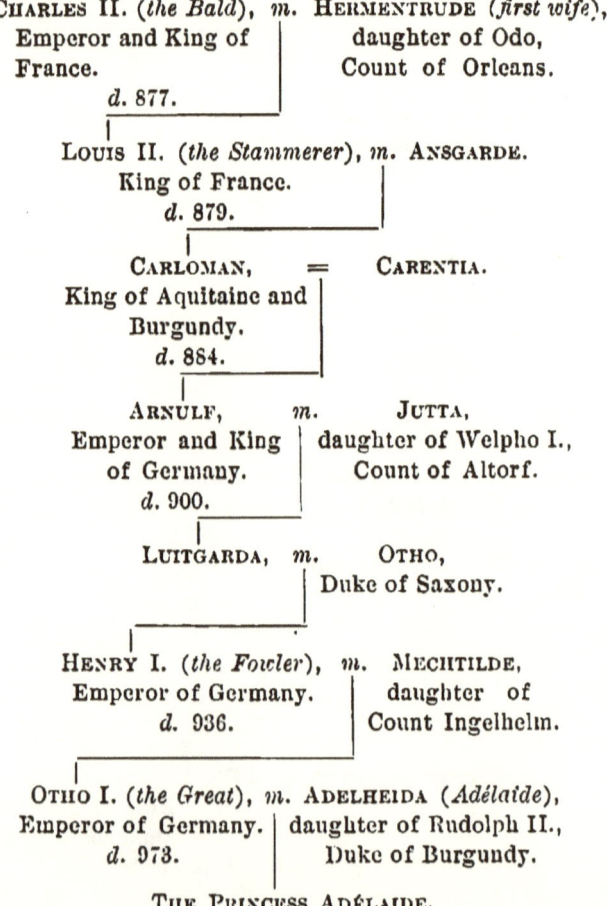

Charles II. (*the Bald*), m. Hermentrude (*first wife*), Emperor and King of France. *d.* 877.   daughter of Odo, Count of Orleans.

Louis II. (*the Stammerer*), m. Ansgarde. King of France. *d.* 879.

Carloman, = Carentia. King of Aquitaine and Burgundy. *d.* 884.

Arnulf, m. Jutta, Emperor and King of Germany. *d.* 900.   daughter of Welpho I., Count of Altorf.

Luitgarda, m. Otho, Duke of Saxony.

Henry I. (*the Fowler*), m. Mechtilde, Emperor of Germany. *d.* 936.   daughter of Count Ingelhelm.

Otho I. (*the Great*), m. Adelheida (*Adélaide*), Emperor of Germany. *d.* 973.   daughter of Rudolph II., Duke of Burgundy.

The Princess Adélaide.

Note. — Adelheida, or Adélaide, "the good and beautiful Empress of Germany, was the daughter of Rudolph II., Duke of Burgundy; she was taken from prison to marry the Emperor Otho I., A. D. 951." She died in 999.

XIV.

THE CARLOVINGIANS.

PEPIN OF HERISTAL, called also PEPIN LE GROS, was the stock of the Carlovingian line of French kings. He was grandson by his mother's side to Pepin de Landen, who governed Austrasia in the reign of Dagobert, and stood in the same relation by his father to the famous Arnaud, Archbishop of Metz, who combined in his own person the characters of a warrior, statesman, diplomatist, and prince of the church. Upon the death of Dagobert II., in 680, Ebroin, Mayor of the Palace of Neustria, became the legal governor of the Austrasians, who, however, preferred the hazard of a contest in favor of Pepin to the yoke of the well-known tyrant, and a struggle was then begun, the result of which made Pepin of Heristal the virtual master of the Frank monarchy. While this struggle was in progress, and even after its conclusion, and the assassination of Ebroin, Thierry reigned as the nominal king. Pepin contented himself with the old title, " Mayor of the Palace," and not only propped up Thierry himself, but crowned three of his descendants after him, who, in French history, are called Les Rois Fainéans (*Do-nothing Kings*). The real power was firmly grasped in the hands of Pepin, who subdued the tributary princes by continual victories, and consolidated the order of the state without daring to assume the pageantry of it. He died in 714.

CHARLES-MARTEL, the natural son of Pepin of Heristal, succeeded his father, and took the next step in advance, which consisted in administering the kingdom, not with the title of king, but that of "Mayor of the Palace," and the throne absolutely vacant. Throughout his administration he heroically resisted the Saracens and checked the progress of their power. He died in 741.

PEPIN LE BREF (*the Short*), so named on account of his short stature, son of Charles-Martel, was the first king of France of the Carlovingian dynasty. He succeeded to his father's authority conjointly with his brother Carloman, and, by filling the throne with Childeric, a foolish prince of the Merovingian line, surnamed "*the Idiot*," acquired the sanction necessary to support the continued assumption of power by his own family. In 746 Carloman retired to a monastry and Pepin was left without a competitor. The pope and the clergy were easily conciliated in favor of a power which promised to preserve the church from the surrounding anarchy and stop the progress of the Saracens which had spread as far as the south of France. In 750, therefore, Childeric was dethroned, and shortly afterwards Pepin and his queen, Bertha, were crowned by the pope in the Church of St. Denis. The king then accompanied the pope on his return into Italy at the head of an army, and besieging Astolphus, king of the Lombards, in Pavia, compelled him to abandon his pretensions to the sovereignty of Rome and the exarchate of Ravenna. Pepin also was victorious in his wars with the Saracens, united Aquitaine to his kingdom, and waged successful war against the German princes. He died in 768.

CHARLEMAGNE. "This illustrious prince, the restorer of order and obedience in a state of society when only the most commanding talents and heroic steadfastness of purpose could have availed him in a struggle against anarchy and ignorance in their worst forms, was the grandson of Charles-Martel, and lived 742–814, master of an empire which embraced all France, a part of Spain, more than half of Italy, and nearly all Germany. To feel his greatness adequately it must be remembered that all the ancient landmarks of social order had been overthrown with the colossal Roman power, and that the whole civilized world was covered with its ruins and infested with its crimes. The ancient seat of empire was divided among a score of petty tyrants; the Saracens had overrun Spain and threatened the farther West; the northern kingdoms were only known as the cradle of adventurous armies, whose leaders in after years organized the feudal governments of Europe; Russia did not even exist; and England was just emerging from the confusion of the Heptarchy. Some two centuries before, 507–511, Clovis had founded the Frankish monarchy and established himself at Paris, but his power was that of an absolute military chief, and he was succeeded by a line of phantom kings, whose action is scarcely distinguishable from that of the barbarous fermentation proceeding around them. At length Pepin-Heristal and his son, Charles-Martel, slowly paved the way for a new authority, the former by familiarizing men's minds with justice and goodness in the sovereign, and the latter by his heroic resistance of the Saracens, and the promise of an irresistible power in the government. The successes of Charlemagne were the natural issue of these circumstances under the command of his ambition and vast genius, favored by the compliance of the popes, who were willing to encourage a Christian protectorate in the West as a counterpoise to the eastern empire of Irene, and the dreaded power of Haroun-al-Raschid. A catalogue of the principal events and dates is all that we can give in the space to which we are limited. In 768

Charles succeeded to the government conjointly with his brother, Carloman ; and on the death of the latter, in 771, he became sole master of France by wisely refusing to divide the authority with his nephews. In 770 he subdued the revolt of Aquitaine. In 772 he marched against the still idolatrous Saxons, and commenced a conflict which he maintained for upwards of thirty years. In 773 he crossed the Alps, and was shortly crowned King of Lombardy, and acknowledged suzerain of Italy by the pope, with the right of confirming the papal elections. In 778 he carried his arms into Spain, and pursued his victorious career as far as the Elbro, but was surprised on his return in the pass of Roncesvalles, where many of his knights perished, and among the rest Orlando, or Roland, his nephew, the hero of Ariosto. In 780 Louis-le-Débonnaire, his youngest son, was crowned by the pope King of Aquitaine, and Pepin, his second son, King of Lombardy, both at Rome. Between 780 and 782 he visited a terrible retribution upon the Saxons, and compelled their chief to accept the Christian baptism. Towards 790 we find him establishing seminaries of learning, and doing all in his power to elevate the character of the clergy, the most of whom had hitherto known little but the Lord's prayer, besides engaging in projects for the acceleration of commerce, the general improvement of the people, and the promotion of science. Before the end of the century he had invaded Pannonia, and extended his dominions in this direction to the mountains of Bohemia and the Raab. In 800 he was crowned at Rome, 'Emperor of the West' * ; and in 803 was negotiating a union with Irene

---

* "On Christmas day in the last year of the eighth century, Charles sat in the seat of state, hearing mass, which was celebrated by the pope himself at the Vatican. All the greatest Franks and Romans were there. Suddenly the pontiff stepped forward to the king, poured on his head the holy

in order to consolidate the Eastern and Western empires, when the empress was dethroned and exiled by Nicephorus. From this period to his death, which took place at Aix-la-Chapelle, in the seventy-first year of his age, and the forty-seventh of his reign, he was engaged in fortifying the coasts of France against the Northmen, and various matters relating to the security and prosperity of the empire, including the settlement of the succession.

"In person and manners Charlemagne was the perfection of simplicity, modesty, frugality, and, in a word, of true greatness; and, though he was too much given to the society of women, he had the reputation of a good father, a tender husband, and a generous friend. He was indefatigable in all the duties of government, and whether in the camp or the court, had fixed hours for study, in which he took care to engage his courtiers by forming them into an academy. 'For shame,' he exclaimed to one who came before him attired more elegantly than the occasion demanded; 'dress yourself like a man, and if you would be distinguished, let it be by your merits, not by your garments.' His nearest friend and companion was the illustrious Alcuyn, and his fame was so widely spread that the only man, perhaps, of kindred genius of that age, the great caliph, Haroun-al-Raschid, courted his good will, and complimented him by an embassage bearing presents. Before his death he confirmed the succession in the person of his son Louis, by an august ceremony. Placing the imperial crown upon the altar, he ordered Louis to take it with his own hands, that he might understand that he wore it in his own right, under no authority but that of God.

---

oil, and crowned him with a golden crown. The crowd, not untutored to be ready for the occasion, cried, 'To Charles Augustus crowned of God, great and peaceful emperor of the Romans, life and victory!'" (*Kitchin.*)

"Perhaps we cannot conclude better, by way of further illustrating the character of Charlemagne, than with his words of advice to this prince : 'Love your people as your children,' said he ; 'choose your magistrates and governors from those whose belief in God will preserve them from corruption, and see that your own life is blameless.'"   (*Elihu Rich.*)

LOUIS I., called "*the Pious*," or "*le Débonnaire*," was thirty-five years old when he succeeded his father. "His life, almost from the cradle, had been spent in war and government, first under wise and prudent guardians, then under a wise and prudent wife. His father had been a conqueror, a queller of pagans, fierce of temper, a man of blood; he would be a man of peace, building up instead of pulling down, and ruling of all men equally. His father's court had been learned, but full of rudeness and iniquity; his court should be learned also, but refined and pure. His father had crushed the great lords; he would raise them, and govern by them. The clergy should have high authority. The free Franks had sunk to serfdom; he would lift them out of the mire, and recreate a strong and faithful people as a counterpoise to the lords. Thus did he begin his reign." * But these virtues were his dangers. Amiable and pliable, he forgave when a more prudent man would have crushed. In consequence, the great domain welded together by his father, began to break to pieces. In 840, after passing a great portion of his life in a wretched struggle with his sons, he died, and the whole fabric of the empire of Charlemagne broke asunder.

"He was of middle stature, with eyes large and clear, face bright and intelligent, his nose long and straight, his

---

* Kitchin's History of France.

lips fairly thick, perhaps not firm enough in their setting. He was strong-chested, broad-shouldered, very powerful of arm; no man could better handle bow or lance. He was straight-handed, straight-fingered : his legs long and shapely ; his feet long; his voice manly." *

He married first Hermentrude, and after her death Judith, of the house of Guelph, "a lady of exceeding beauty, clever, and ambitious." †

His sons by his first marriage were : —

> HLOTHAR (*Lothaire*), Emperor and King of Italy. Died in 835.
> PEPIN. Died in 838.
> HLUDWIG (*Louis*), King of Bavaria. Succeeded his brother as Emperor and King of Italy. Died in 875.

By his wife Judith an only son was born : —

> CHARLES II. (*the Bald*), born in 823; King of France.

CHARLES II., called "*the Bald*," King of France, was a man of some gifts, and was ambitious. After the death of his half brothers, he attempted to restore the empire, and succeeded in getting himself crowned King of Italy by the pope. He had begun an intrigue with the German nobles, when, at the request of the pope, who was hard pressed by the Saracens and other foes, he dropped his projects against Germany and prepared an expedition into Italy. While leading this expedition death overtook him. He died in 877 in a dilapidated hut on Mont Cenis. His daughter, Judith, by his second wife, Richeldis of Burgundy, was married to Æthelwulf of England. After the death of Æthelwulf she married Baldwin I., Count of Flanders.‡

---

* Thegan, Opus de Gestis Ludovici Pii Imp. c. 19.
† Kitchin's History of France.
‡ See " II. Æthelwulf," page 25, and " Count Baldwin I.," page 49.

XV.

THE CAPETIANS.

ROBERT, surnamed "*the Strong*," is regarded as the stock of the Capet Dynasty. He died in 866.

ROBERT, his son, received the crown of France at Soissons, in 922, from the lords opposed to Charles the Simple. He was killed in 923.

HUGH THE GREAT, his son, Duke of France and Burgundy, and Count of Paris and Orleans, was never crowned. He died in 956.

HUGH-CAPET,* his son, was the founder of the third dynasty of the kings of France. He was born in 939, crowned at Rheims in 987. He died in 996, and was succeeded by his son.

ROBERT, surnamed "*the Pious*," shared the throne with his father from 988 to 996, when he succeeded as the sole king. He died in 1031. His daughter, Adalais (Alice), by his wife, Constance of Provence, was married to Baldwin V., Count of Flanders, and was the mother of Matilda, of Flanders, the wife of William the Conqueror.†

---

* The name Capet is thought to come from the "cape," "chape," or "cap," the hood of St. Martin, which Hugh always wore, declining to wear a crown. "Capetus, *i. q.* Cappotus." Others say he was so named from the size of his head.

† See page 49.

XVI.

THE DESCENT OF BARBARA LUCY

FROM THE PRINCESS GUNDRED, THROUGH THE EARLS OF WARREN
AND SURREY, THE EARLS OF NORFOLK, THE LORDS DE
HASTINGS, AND THE LORDS DE GREY DE RUYTHN.

I. "**WILLIAM DE WARRENNE,** Earl of Warrenne,
in Normandy, a near kinsman of William the Conqueror,
came into England with that prince, and, having distinguished himself at the battle of Hastings, obtained an
immense portion of the public spoliation. He had large
grants of lands in several counties, among which were the
Barony of Lewes, in Sussex, and the manors of Carletune
and Beningtun, in Lincolnshire. So extensive, indeed, were
those grants, that his possessions resembled more the dominions of a sovereign prince than the estates of a subject.
He enjoyed, too, in the highest degree, the confidence of the
king, and was appointed joint justice-general with Richard
de Benefactis, for administering justice throughout the
whole realm. While in that office, some great disturbers of
the public peace having refused to appear before him and his
colleague, in obedience to citation, the Earl took up arms
and defeated the rebels in a battle at Fagadune, when, he is
said, for the purpose of striking terror, to have cut off the
right foot of each of his prisoners. Of these rebels, Ralph
Wahir, or Guader, Earl of Norfolk, and Roger, Earl of
Hereford, were the ringleaders. His lordship was likewise highly esteemed by King William Rufus, and was
created by that monarch Earl of Surrey. He married
GUNDRED, daughter of the CONQUEROR, and had issue." *

---

* Burke's Dormant, Forfeited, and Extinct Peerages of the British
Empire.

WILLIAM, his successor.

REGINALD, one of the adherents of Robert Curthose.

GUNDRED-EDITH, married, first, to Girard de Garnay, and, second, to Drew de Monceax.

Another daughter was married to Ernise de Colungis.

The Princess Gundred (Countess of Warrenne and Surrey) died at Castle Acre, in 1085, and was buried in the Chapter House of Lewes Priory. William de Warrenne (Earl of Warrenne and Surrey) died in 1089.

II. **WILLIAM DE WARRENNE,** Earl of Warrenne and second Earl of Surrey. This nobleman joined Robert de Belesmé, Earl of Arundel and Shrewsbury, in favor of Robert Curthose, against Henry I., and in consequence forfeited his English earldom and estates. These were subsequently restored to him, and he became a good and faithful subject to King Henry. His lordship married ISABEL DE VERMANDOIS, widow of Robert, Earl of Mellent, and daughter of HUGH-MAGNUS,* Count de Vermandois, by whom he had issue.

WILLIAM, his successor.

REGINALD, who, marrying Alice, daughter and heir of William de Wirmgay, became Lord of Wirmgay, in Norfolk.

RALPH.

GUNDRED, married first to Roger de Newburgh, Earl of Warwick, and second to William de Lancaster, Baron of Kendal.

ADELINE, married to Henry, son of David, King of Scotland.

The Earl died May 11, 1138, and was succeeded by his eldest son.

III. **WILLIAM DE WARRENNE,** Earl of Warrenne, and third Earl of Surrey, zealously espoused the cause of

---

* Eastern ancestry of Hugh Magnus, see page 69.

King Stephen, and held a high command in the army of that monarch in the battle fought at Lincoln between him and the adherents of the Empress Maud. His lordship married ADELA, daughter of WILLIAM TALVACE, son of ROBERT DE BELESMÉ, Earl of Shrewsbury, and by her had an only daughter and heir, Isabel.

In 1147 the Earl assumed the cross, and accompanied Louis VII., King of France, on a crusade against the Saracens in the Holy Land. From this expedition he never returned.

IV. **ISABEL DE WARREN,** Countess of Surrey, married first, William de Blois, a natural son of King Stephen, who became, in consequence, Earl of Surrey. This nobleman was with Henry II. at the siege of Thoulouse, and died there in 1160, leaving no heirs. His widow, Isabel, married in 1163 HAMELINE PLANTAGENET, natural brother of King Henry II., who obtained, *jure uxoris*, the Earldom of Surrey, and assumed the surname and arms of DE WARREN. This nobleman bore one of the three swords at the second coronation of Richard I., and served with distinction in the army of that monarch in Normandy. He died May 7, 1202, four years after the countess, having issue.

> WILLIAM, his successor.
> ADELA, wife of Sir William Fitzwilliam.
> MAUD, who probably died unmarried.
> *A daughter,* wife of Gilbert de Aquila.
> ISABEL, wife of Roger, Earl of Norfolk.
> MARGARET, wife of Baldwin, Earl of Devon.

V. **LADY ISABEL PLANTAGENET** was married to ROGER BIGOD, the second Earl of Norfolk. In the first year of the reign of Richard I. this nobleman was sent as an ambassador from the English monarch to Philip of

France, for the purpose of obtaining aid in carrying on a crusade against the Saracens in the Holy Land. "Upon the return of King Richard from his captivity, the Earl of Norfolk assisted at the great council held by the king at Nottingham; and at his second coronation his lordship was one of the four earls that carried the silken canopy over the monarch's head. In the reign of King John he was one of the barons that extorted the great CHARTERS OF FREEDOM from that prince, and was amongst the twenty-five lords appointed to enforce their fulfilment."

The Earl died in 1220 and was succeeded by his eldest son. His children by his wife, Lady Isabel, were, —

> HUGH, his successor, who married Maud, daughter of William Mareschal, Earl of Pembroke.
>
> WILLIAM, who married Margaret, daughter of Robert de Sutton.
>
> THOMAS, who probably died unmarried.
>
> MARGERY, wife of William de Hastings.
>
> ADELIZA, wife of Alberic de Vere, Earl of Oxford.
>
> MARY, wife of Ralph Fitz-Robert, Lord of Middleham.

VI. **LADY MARGERY BIGOD,** the eldest daughter, was married to WILLIAM DE HASTINGS, son of WILLIAM DE HASTINGS (*steward to King Henry II.*) and his wife MAUD, daughter of THURSTAN BANASTER. William de Hastings, the father, was Lord of Fillongley, County of Warwick, and was the possessor of the manors of Aston-Flamville, County of Leicester, and Grissing, in Norfolk.

VII. **HENRY DE HASTINGS,** the only child of William by his wife Margery, married ADA,* daughter of DAVID, Earl of Huntingdon, and of MAUD, his wife, daughter of HUGH, Earl of Chester, and one of the sisters and co-heiresses of Ranulph, Earl of Chester, and through her he eventu-

---

* Ancestry of Lady Ada. See "The Scottish Line," pages 70, 71.

ally shared in the great estates of the earls of Chester. By this lady he had issue, — one son and two daughters.

HENRY, his heir and successor.
MARGERY.
HILLARIA.

This Henry de Hastings attended King Henry III. into France in the twenty-sixth year of that monarch's reign (1241), was taken prisoner at the great defeat which the English army sustained at Zante, but was soon after released. A few years afterward he accompanied Richard, Earl of Cornwall, into France, whither the said earl proceeded at that period with a splendid retinue, but for what purpose does not appear. About the close of the same year, 1250, Henry de Hastings died,* and was succeeded by his son.

VIII. **HENRY DE HASTINGS,** being a minor at the time of his father's death, his wardship was granted to Guy de Lazinian,† a half brother to King Henry III. This Henry de Hastings, in the forty-fourth year of the reign of Henry III. (1259), was summoned to be at Shrewsbury, with horse and arms, to march against the Welsh; and in the year following received a similar summons to be at London. Soon afterwards, however, we find him, with other turbulent spirits, in arms against the king, under the banner of Simon de Montfort, Earl of Leicester. In consequence he was, with the other rebellious nobles, excommunicated by the Archbishop of Canterbury. He became one of the most zealous of the baronial leaders, and distinguished himself at the battle of Lewes, wherein the king was made prisoner.

---

* At the time of the decease of this Henry de Hastings, his two daughters, Margery and Hillaria, were in the nunnery of Alneston, and their tuition was then committed to William de Cantelupe.

† See "The Family of William de Lusignan (de Valence), Earl of Pembroke," page 80.

As a reward, he received the honor of knighthood at the hands of Montfort, and was appointed governor of Scarborough and Winchester castles. He died in 1264, and was succeeded by his son.

IX.   HENRY DE HASTINGS, who married LADY JOAN DE CANTELUPE, daughter of BARON WILLIAM DE CANTELUPE, and sister and at length co-heir of George de Cantelupe, Baron of Abergavenny, and had issue, — three sons and three daughters.

> JOHN.
> EDMUND.
> EDWARD.
> AUDRA.
> LORA.
> JOAN.

This feudal lord was summoned to Parliament, as Baron Hastings, December 14, 1264. He died in 1268, and was succeeded by his eldest son.

X.   JOHN DE HASTINGS (*second baron*) was summoned to Parliament as Lord Hastings, from June 23, 1295, to May 22, 1313. This nobleman was a distinguished military leader during the reign of Edward I. In the twelfth year of the reign of that monarch (1283), he accompanied the expedition to Scotland. In 1286 he was in Wales with Edmund, Earl of Cornwall, who was regent of the kingdom during the king's absence in Gascony. Subsequently, he took part in an expedition sent into Ireland, and in 1301 he was again in Scotland, where he performed military service for five knights' fees. In the following year (31 Edward I.) he rendered important service at the celebrated siege of Kaerlaverock, carried on by Edward, Prince of Wales. Three years afterwards (34 Edward I.), as a

reward for his efficient military service, he was given by the king a grant of the whole of the County of Menteith, with the islands, and also the manors and lands of Alan, Earl of Menteith, then declared an enemy and rebel to the king. He was also made Seneschal of Aquitaine. In 1290 he was one of the competitors for the crown of Scotland, in right of his descent from Ada, daughter of David, Earl of Hunt-ingdon, brother of Malcolm and William, kings of Scotland.* His lordship married, first, Lady Isabel,† daughter of William de Valence, Earl of Pembroke, half brother of King Henry III., and sister and co-heir of Aymer de Valence, Earl of Pembroke. Lady Isabel died October 3, 1305. Two of their children were : —

> John, his heir and successor.
> Elizabeth, wife of Roger, Lord Grey.

He married a second wife, Lady Isabel, daughter of Hugh Despencer, Earl of Winchester, and by her had two sons. His lordship died in 1313.

XI. **LADY ELIZABETH HASTINGS,** married Roger de Grey,‡ a son of John de Grey (*Baron Grey of Condor*). This Roger de Grey was summoned to Parliament from December 30, 1324 (18 Edward II.), to November 15, 1351 (25 Edward III.), as Lord Grey de Ruthyn. He died in 1353.

XII. **REGINALD DE GREY,** his son and heir, was summoned to Parliament from March 15, 1354 (28 Edward

---

* Two of the other principal competitors were John de Baliol and Robert de Bruce. See "The Scottish Line," page 71.

† See "The family of William de Lusignan (de Valence), Earl of Pembroke," page 80.

‡ Descent of Roger de Grey, see "The Greys," pages 73–75.

III.), to March 20, 1388 (11 Richard II.), as Reginald de Grey de Ruthyn. He married ELIZABETH, a daughter of ROGER, fourth BARON LE STRANGE, of Knokyn, and had issue. His lordship died in 1388.

XIII.   REGINALD DE GREY,* his son and heir, was summoned to Parliament from October 6, 1389 (13 Richard II.), to September 26, 1439 (18 Henry VI.), as Reginald de Grey de Ruthyn.   His lordship married LADY JOANE,† only daughter of WILLIAM DE ASTLEY, fourth Lord Astley.   He died in 1440, leaving four children by his wife Joane.

> EDWARD, Lord Ferrers, of Groby, summoned to Parliament in 1446.
> JOHN DE GREY, of Barwell, in the County of Leicester.
> ROBERT DE GREY, of Enville and Whitington, in the County of Stafford.
> ELEANOR, wife of William Lucy.

XIV.   LADY ELEANOR DE GREY,‡ the daughter, married WILLIAM LUCY of Charlecote, in the County of Warwick.   It was this William Lucy who, during his mi-

---

* "In 13 Richard II., that monarch keeping his Christmas at Woodstock, his lordship (John Hastings, third Earl of Pembroke), only then seventeen years of age, adventuring to tilt with Sir John St. John, was so severely wounded by an unlucky slip of Sir John's lance, in the abdomen, that he died almost immediately, 30th December, 1389, when leaving no issue, the Earldom of Pembroke became extinct. At his lordship's thus premature decease, Reginald, Lord Grey de Ruthyn (grandson of Roger, Lord Grey, and his wife, Elizabeth Hastings), was found to be his heir of the whole blood."

† Lady Joane was his lordship's second wife. Lady Joane's ancestry, see "The Astleys of Astley," pages 76-79.

‡ In Burke's "History of the Commoners," Lady Eleanor's name is written "Elizabeth," but in the records of the Greys de Ruthyn she is called "Eleanor." See "XVI. William Lucy," page 91.

nority, was in ward to John Boteler of Warrington, and
who, upon the decease of Lady Elizabeth Clinton, 1423,
was found to be her cousin and next heir. In the war of
the Roses, William Lucy arrayed himself under the banner
of the House of York. He died in 1466, and was succeeded
by his son.

XV. **SIR WILLIAM LUCY,** of Charlecote, created a
Knight of the Bath at the coronation of the queen of Henry
VII. He married, first, MARGARET, daughter of JOHN
BRECKNOCK, treasurer to King Henry VI., and, secondly,
Alice, daughter of William Hanbury. He died in 1492.

XVI. **EDWARD LUCY,** of Charlecote, his son by the
first wife, born in 1464, was a soldier of high repute in the
reign of Henry VII., for we find him in command of a
division of the royal army at the battle of Stoke, and afterwards retained to serve the king in the French Wars. In
1494 he was summoned, with other persons of rank, to
attend the creation of the king's son, the Duke of York, at
which ceremony he was to be made a Knight of the Bath.
But it seems he did not appear, for in April, of the year
following, his testament bears date, and in that he is styled
Esquire. He married, first, Elizabeth, daughter and
heiress of Walter Tramsington, by whom he had no issue,
and, secondly, JANE, daughter of RICHARD LUDLOW, and
was succeeded at his decease (the probate of his last will
and testament being 19th May, 1498 (14 Henry VII.), by
his eldest son.

XVII. **SIR THOMAS LUCY,** Knt., of Charlecote, one
of the servers to King Henry VIII. He married ELIZABETH,
widow of George Catesby of Ashby-Legers, in the County

of Northampton, and daughter of SIR RICHARD EMPSON, Knt., by whom he had issue.

> WILLIAM, his heir and successor.
>
> THOMAS, upon whom his father settled the manor of Cleybrooke, in Leicestershire.
>
> EDMUND, who inherited the manors of Beckering and Sharpenho.
>
> ANNE, wife of Thomas Herbert.
>
> RADIGUND, wife of —— Betts.
>
> BARBARA, wife of RICHARD TRACY, of Stanway, Gloucestershire.

Sir Thomas Lucy died in 1525, and was succeeded by his eldest son.

NOTE. — During the first year of the reign of Queen Elizabeth, Sir Thomas Lucy, son of Sir William, and nephew of Barbara, rebuilt the manor house at Charlecote, as it now stands. It was this Sir Thomas Lucy who prosecuted Shakespeare for stealing deer from Fulbroke Park. The prosecution was conducted with much bitterness, in consequence of a lampoon which the poet had written on Sir Thomas. As a result, Shakespeare was compelled to fly from his native place, in order to escape the consequences. The great dramatist, however, revenged himself by subsequently delineating Sir Thomas under the character of "Justice Shallows."

XVII.

THE EASTERN ANCESTRY OF HUGH-MAGNUS.

ANCESTOR OF BARBARA LUCY, WIFE OF RICHARD TRACY OF STANWAY.

ROMANUS II.,
Emperor of the East,
r. 959-63.
Grandson of Constantine X.

ANNE, *m.* WOLODOMIR,
Grand Duke of Russia.

JAROSLAUS,
Grand Duke of Russia.

ANNE, *m.* HENRY I.,
King of France.
r. 1031-1060.

HUGH-MAGNUS,*
Count de Vermandois.

---

* See "II. William de Warrenne," page 60.

XVIII.

THE SCOTTISH LINE.*

ANCESTORS OF LADY ADA, WIFE OF HENRY DE HASTINGS, AND OF
BARBARA LUCY, WIFE OF RICHARD TRACY OF STANWAY.

KENNETH II., son of McAlpine, subdued the fierce Picts to submission under the same sceptre as the Scots. He was the founder of the Scottish monarchy, and reigned from 843 to 858.

CONSTANTINE II., his son, reigned as king of Scotland from 862 to 878. It was during his reign that the Danes invaded Scotland. He was taken prisoner by them in 878, and was beheaded at a place called "The Devil's Cave."

DONALD IV., his son, reigned prosperously from 892 to 903, and did much to civilize Scotland. He died a natural death.

MALCOLM I., his son, reigned from 943 to 958. He was killed while trying to quell an insurrection at Mearns.

KENNETH III., his son, reigned from 970 to 994, when he was assassinated at the instigation of Lady Fenella.

MALCOLM II., his son, reigned from 1003 to 1033, when he was murdered by his cousin.

THE PRINCESS BEATRIX, his daughter, married GRIMUS, governor of the Scotch islands, and the crown passed to their son.

DUNCAN I., their son, succeeded his grandfather and reigned from 1033 to 1034, when he was murdered by his cousin, Macbeth.

---

* See Fitzgerald's Kings of Europe. London. 1870.

MALCOLM III., his son, succeeded to the crown in 1056 and reigned until 1093. He married MARGARET,* a daughter of EDWARD, son of EDMUND IRONSIDES, King of England. Margaret was the first crowned queen of Scotland, and a most amiable and excellent woman.

DAVID I. (*St. David*), their son, came to the throne in 1124 and reigned until 1153. He married MAUD, a daughter of the EARL OF NORTHUMBERLAND and JUDITH, his wife, niece of William the Conqueror. Their son, Henry, died during the life of his father, and the crown passed to a grandson, — son of Henry.

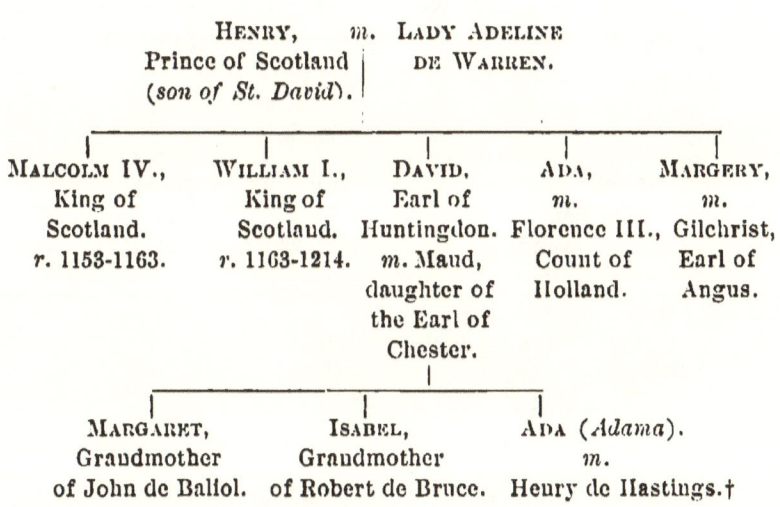

HENRY, *m.* LADY ADELINE
Prince of Scotland | DE WARREN.
(*son of St. David*).

MALCOLM IV.,	WILLIAM I.,	DAVID,	ADA,	MARGERY,
King of	King of	Earl of	*m.*	*m.*
Scotland.	Scotland.	Huntingdon.	Florence III.,	Gilchrist,
r. 1153-1163.	*r.* 1163-1214.	*m.* Maud,	Count of	Earl of
		daughter of	Holland.	Angus.
		the Earl of		
		Chester.		

MARGARET,	ISABEL,	ADA (*Adama*).
Grandmother	Grandmother	*m.*
of John de Baliol.	of Robert de Bruce.	Henry de Hastings.†

---

* Ancestry of Margaret, see page 72.
† See " VII. Henry de Hastings," page 62.

XIX.

THE DESCENT OF MARGARET,

Wife of Malcolm III., the First Crowned Queen of Scotland, Ancestress of Lady Ada, Wife of Henry de Hastings, and of Barbara Lucy, Wife of Richard Tracy of Stanway.

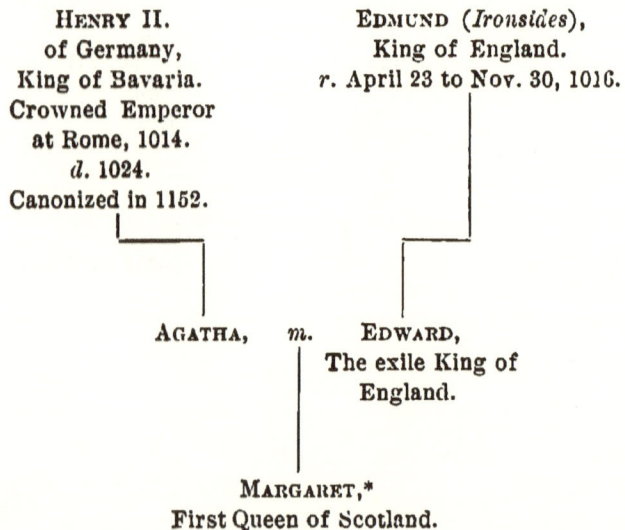

HENRY II.
of Germany,
King of Bavaria.
Crowned Emperor
at Rome, 1014.
d. 1024.
Canonized in 1152.

EDMUND (*Ironsides*),
King of England.
r. April 23 to Nov. 30, 1016.

AGATHA,   *m*.   EDWARD,
The exile King of
England.

MARGARET,*
First Queen of Scotland.

---

* See " Malcolm III.," page 71.

XX.

THE GREYS,

ANCESTORS OF ROGER DE GREY, LORD GREY DE RUTHYN, AND OF
BARBARA LUCY, WIFE OF RICHARD TRACY OF STANWAY.

I. **HENRY DE GREY.** The manor of Thurrock, in the
County of Essex, was conferred upon this Henry de Grey
by King Richard I., in the sixth year of his reign (1194).
This grant was afterwards confirmed by King John, who
vouchsafed, by special charter, to permit the said Henry
de Grey to hunt the hare and fox in any land belonging to
the crown, save the king's own demesne parks. In 1216
King Henry III. gave him the manor of Grimston, in the
County of Nottingham. He married ISOLDA, niece and
heiress of Robert Bardolf, and shared in the inheritance of
his lands.

II. **SIR JOHN DE GREY,** his second son, held the
office of Sheriff for the counties of Buckingham and Bedford (1233). In the twenty-sixth year of the reign of
Henry III. (1241), he was summoned, with horse and
arms, to attend the king upon the expedition then made
into Flanders.

"In the 35 Henry III. the Lady Joane, widow of Pauline Pevere, a
great man in that age, being possessed of all her husband's estates, sold
to this John the marriage of her son for 500 marks, he undertaking to
discharge her of any fine to the king; whereupon he married him to his
own daughter; and when this Joane heard that the king had given her in
marriage (as she was a widow) to one Stephen de Salines, an alien, she,
by the advice of her friends, matched herself to this John de Grey, which
being told to the king, he grew much offended, but at length accepted of a
fine of 500 marks from him for that transgression." (*Dugdale.*)

In 1252, Sir John de Grey was appointed governor of Northampton Castle, and the next year he was made Steward of all Gascony. Four years afterwards he was nominated to the governorship of Shrewsbury Castle, and constable of that of Dover. In 1262 he was Sheriff of Herefordshire and governor of Hereford Castle. The next year he had the custody of all the lands of Anker de Frescheville, in the counties of Nottingham and Derby. He was one of the noblemen who undertook that the king should abide by the arbitration of Louis IX. (*Saint Louis*) of France, touching the misunderstanding with the barons. But, remaining loyal to the king (*Henry III.*) throughout the armed resistance, he was appointed, after the victory of Evesham, Sheriff of the counties of Nottingham and Derby. Sir John died in 1265, and was succeeded by his son.

III. **REGINALD DE GREY,** his son, in consideration of his faithful services to the king, obtained " special livery " of all his father's lands, although at that time he had not "done his homage." In 1280 (*reign of Edward I.*) he was made the Justice of Chester, and in this office he so satisfactorily served the king, that, as a reward, he was given a part of the "Honour of Monmouth, the Castle of Ruthyn, and other lands." In 1293 he was summoned to be at Portsmouth, to attend the king in Gascony, then menaced by the French. During the following year he was summoned to Parliament as a baron. In 1296, when the government of England was committed to Prince Edward, during the king's absence in Flanders, he was appointed assistant to the prince. During the same year he was one of the sureties, on the part of the king, for the observance of the charters. Afterwards we find him taking a prominent part in the wars of Scotland.

His lordship married MAUD, daughter and heiress of WILLIAM, LORD FITZ-HUGH, by HAWYS, daughter and heiress of HUGH DE LONGCHAMP, of Wilton Castle, in the County of Hereford, which came into the family of Grey by this marriage.

IV. **JOHN DE GREY,** his eldest son (*second baron*), was summoned to Parliament from June 9, 1309, to September 18, 1322. In 1316 (10 *Edward II.*) he was made the Justice of North Wales and governor of the Castle of Caernarvon. His lordship married, first, Anne, daughter of William, Lord Ferrers, of Groby; and, second, MAUD, daughter of RALPH, LORD BASSET.

V. **ROGER DE GREY,** his eldest son by the second wife, was summoned to Parliament as Lord Grey de Ruthyn. He married LADY ELIZABETH HASTINGS.*

---

* See " XI. Lady Elizabeth Hastings," page 65.

XXI.

THE ASTLEYS OF ASTLEY,

ANCESTORS OF LADY JOANE DE ASTLEY, WIFE OF REGINALD, LORD
GREY DE RUTHYN; AND OF BARBARA LUCY, WIFE OF RICHARD
TRACY OF STANWAY.

This noble family derived its surname from the MANOR
OF ASTLEY, formerly written *Estley*, in the County of Warwick, which, with other estates in that shire, belonged to
the Astleys at the beginning of the reign of King Henry I.

I. **PHILIP DE ESTLEY**, grandson of the first possessor, was, upon the assessment of the aid towards the
marriage portion of the daughter of Henry II., certified
to hold three knights' fees of William, Earl of Warwick,
de veteri Feoffamento, — "by the service of laying hands on
the earl's stirrop when he did get upon or alight from horse-
back." This feudal baron was succeeded by his son.

II. **THOMAS DE ASTLEY** of Astley, held certain
lands of the "Honour of Leicester" and became a kind of
bailiff to Simon de Montfort, Earl of Leicester. In 1210
(12 *John*) this Thomas de Astley paid a hundred marks to
the crown, "to be excused from going beyond the sea," — it
is supposed in a military expedition into Ireland. A few
years afterwards we find him and other dissatisfied noblemen
in arms against the king. In 1215 (17 *John*), he was committed a prisoner to Bedford Castle, and his estates were
confiscated by the crown. When Henry III. came to the
throne his territorial possessions were restored to him

(1216), and he returned to his allegiance to the king. In 1218 he was appointed a commissioner for restoring to the crown all the demesnes of which King John was possessed at the beginning of his wars with barons. This feudal lord married MAUD, one of the sisters and co-heirs of Roger de Camvill of Creeke, in the County of Northampton, and was succeeded by his son.

III. **WALTER DE ASTLEY** of Astley, his son, participated, with his father, in the rebellion of the barons against King John. He died before 1240, leaving a son and heir.

IV. **SIR THOMAS DE ASTLEY**, Knt., was for many years a loyal and faithful subject of King Henry III., and from 1241 to 1250 held various appointments under the crown. But in 1262 (47 *Henry III.*), we find him one of the leaders of the rebellious barons who seized upon the revenues of the crown in the counties of Warwick and Leicester. In the following year, when the king submitted to the "Provisions of Oxford," he was nominated "*Custos Pacis*" for Leicestershire. Soon afterwards, in 1264 (49 *Henry III.*), the battle of Evesham was fought between the king and the barons. Montfort, Earl of Leicester, and many other insurrectionary nobles were slain, among them Sir Thomas de Astley. The estates of the family were then confiscated by the crown and conferred upon Warine de Bessingbourne.*

Sir Thomas married, first, JOANE, daughter of ERNALD DE BOIS, a person of great consequence in the County of

---

* "The king, compassionating his widow and children, reserved to them out of these estates certain lands, valued at £34 18s. 1d. per annum."

Leicester; and, second, Editha, daughter of Peter Constable, of Melton Constable, in the County of Norfolk, and sister of Sir Ralph Constable, Knt.

V. **THOMAS DE ASTLEY,** his eldest son by the first marriage, was eventually put into possession of his father's estates by virtue of a decree called *"Dictum de Kenilworth,"* paying as a compensation to Warine de Bessingbourne 320 marks sterling, to raise which sum he sold his manor of Little Copston to the monks of Combe. Subsequently he was engaged in the Scottish war of King Edward I., and participated in the victory of Falkirk. For his loyalty and efficient military service he seems to have been rewarded, as he was summoned to Parliament as Baron Astley * from June 23, 1295, to November 3, 1306. At his decease he was succeeded by his eldest son, Nicholas.

VI. **SIR GUY DE ASTLEY,** the second son, in company with his elder brother, Nicholas, the second Lord Astley, was in the army in Scotland with King Edward II., and both were taken prisoners at Bannocksburn. The date of the decease of Nicholas (Lord Astley) is not known, but, having outlived his brother Sir Guy, and dying issueless, the title and estates devolved upon his nephew, THOMAS, the son and heir of SIR GUY by his wife ALICE, second daughter and co-heiress of SIR THOMAS WOLVEY, Knt.†

---

* The first Lord Astley.

† V. THOMAS,
First Lord Astley.

		SIR THOMAS WOLVEY, Knt.
NICHOLAS,	VI. SIR GUY, *m.*	ALICE.
Second Lord Astley.	*d.* before Nicholas.	
d. issueless.		
	VII. THOMAS,	
	Third Lord Astley.	

VII. **THOMAS DE ASTLEY,** third Lord Astley, was summoned to Parliament from February 25, 1342, to March 10, 1349. This nobleman, unlike his warrior ancestors, was more of a churchman than a soldier. About 1339, in the reign of Edward III., he founded a chantry in the parish church of Astley. Afterwards, obtaining permission to change his chantry priests into a dean and secular canons, he erected a beautiful and substantial collegiate church, in the form of a cross, with a tall spire, and dedicated to the Assumption of the Blessed Virgin. His lordship married ELIZABETH, daughter of GUY DE BEAUCHAMP,* Earl of Warwick, and had issue.

VIII. **WILLIAM DE ASTLEY**, his eldest son, was the fourth Lord Astley, but was never summoned to Parliament. This nobleman was included in several commissions during the reign of Henry IV. and Henry V. His lordship married CATHERINE, daughter of WILLIAM, LORD WILLOUGHBY DE ERESBY, by whom he left an *only daughter* — Joane.

IX. **LADY JOANE DE ASTLEY** married, first, Thomas Raleigh of Farnborough, in the County of Warwick, by whom she had no issue; and, secondly, REGINALD, LORD GREY DE RUTHYN, by whom she had three sons and a daughter.†

---

* See "IX. Guy de Beauchamp," pages 95, 96.
† See "XIII. Reginald de Grey," page 66.

XXII.

THE FAMILY OF WILLIAM DE LUSIGUAN (DE VALENCE), EARL OF PEMBROKE.

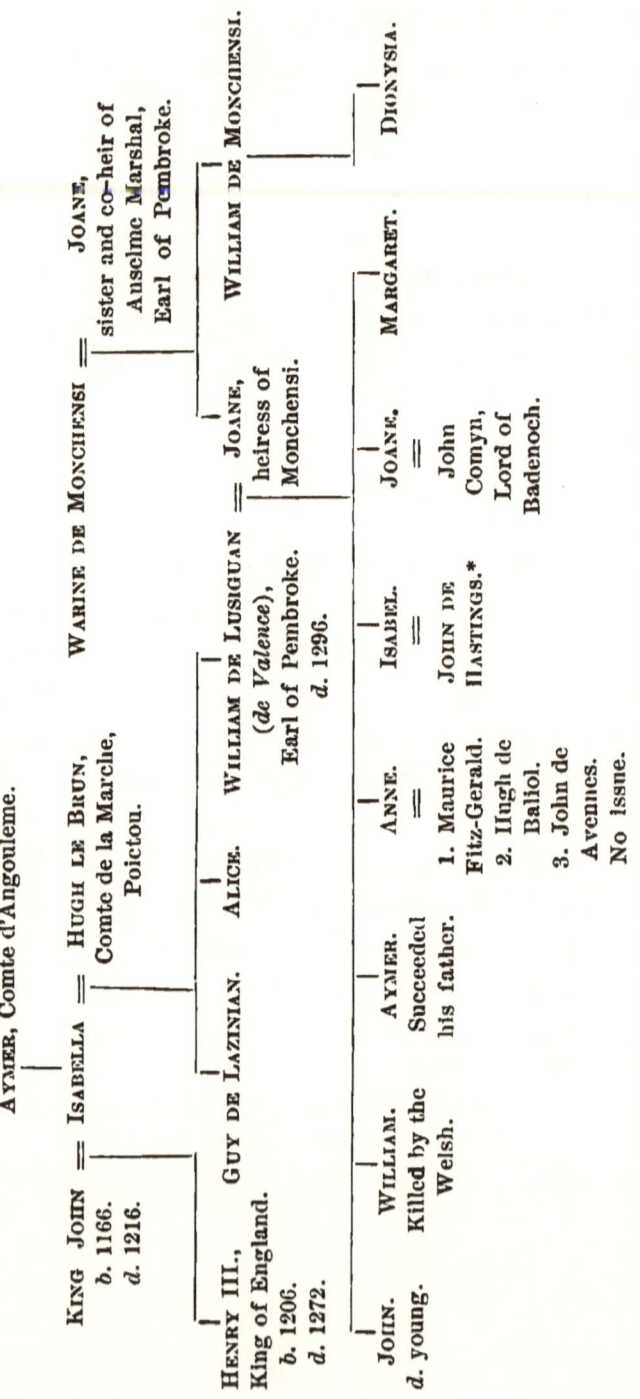

AYMER, Comte d'Angouleme.

KING JOHN = ISABELLA = HUGH LE BRUN,
b. 1166.   Comte de la Marche,
d. 1216.   Poictou.

WARINE DE MONCHENSI = JOANE,
                        sister and co—heir of
                        Anselme Marshal,
                        Earl of Pembroke.

HENRY III.,   GUY DE LAZINIAN.   ALICE.   WILLIAM DE LUSIGUAN = JOANE,   WILLIAM DE MONCHENSI.
King of England.   (*de Valence*),   heiress of
b. 1206.   Earl of Pembroke.   Monchensi.
d. 1272.   *d.* 1296.

JOHN.   WILLIAM.   AYMER.   ANNE.   ISABEL.   JOANE.   MARGARET.   DIONYSIA.
d. young. Killed by the   Succeeded   =   =   =
         Welsh.   his father. 1. Maurice   JOHN DE   John
                                      Fitz-Gerald.   HASTINGS.*   Comyn,
                                      2. Hugh de   Lord of
                                      Baliol.   Badenoch.
                                      3. John de
                                      Avennes.
                                      No Issue.

* See "X. John de Hastings," page 64.

XXIII.

WILLIAM DE LUSIGUAN, OTHERWISE DE VALENCE, EARL OF PEMBROKE.

Inspecting the genealogical chart of "the family of William de Lusiguan (de Valence)," we see that Henry III. of England was the half brother of Guy, William, and Alice, and, because of this relationship and the oppression to which they had been subjected in France, the two brothers and their sister were brought into England, in 1247, and provided for by the English monarch.

This William de Lusiguan, a few months after his arrival in England, was made governor of Goderich Castle, and, through the influence of the king, obtained the hand of Joane, daughter and, eventually, heir of Warine de Monchensi.

"Moreover, shortly after this, the king, solemnizing the festival of St. Edward's translation in the church of Westminster with great state, sitting on the royal throne in a rich robe of baudekyn, and the crown on his head, caused this William (with divers other young noblemen) to be brought before him, and girt him with the sword of knighthood; and, whilst he thus sate in his royal seat, casting his eye upon him who penned down all the particulars of the great solemnity, he called him nearer, and commanded him to sit upon the middle step, betwixt his chair and the floor, and said to him: 'Hast thou taken notice of all these things, and perfectly committed them to memory?' He answered: 'Sir, I have so; deeming this famous ceremonial worthy to be recorded.' Whereupon the king replied: 'I am fully satisfied that God Almighty, as a pledge of his further favors and benefits, hath vouchsafed to work one glorious miracle this morning, for which I give Him thanks. I therefore intreat thee, and intreating require, that thou record these things exactly and fully, and write them in a book, lest that the memory of them should in time be lost'; and, having so said, invited him with whom he had this discourse to dinner that day, with three of his fellows; commanding likewise that all other monks who then came thither, with the whole convent of Westminster, should at this charge be that day feasted at the public refectory there." (*Sir William Dugdale*.)

Subsequently, this William de Lusiguan, or William de Valence as he was called in England, was granted by the crown the Castle and Honour of Hertford. In another grant, made to himself "and his lady and their issue," he was given "all those debts which William de Lancaster did then owe to the Jews throughout the whole realm."

The following illustrates the manner in which this William and other noblemen of the period were in the habit of conducting themselves : —

"About this time, this William de Valence, residing at Hertford Castle, rode to the Park at Haethfel, belonging to the bishop of Ely, and there hunting without any leave, went to the bishop's manor house, and, readily finding nothing to drink but ordinary beer, broke open the buttery doors, and swearing and cursing the drink, and those who made it; after all his company had drunk their fills, pulled the spigots out of the vessels, and let out the rest on the floor; and that a servant of the house hearing the noise, and coming to see what the matter was, they laughed him to scorn, and so departed." (*Sir William Dugdale*.)

In 1249 William de Valence was with the army of the Crusaders in the Holy Land. After his return to England he was summoned by the king (1257) to march against the

Welsh. Soon afterwards, however, he was obliged to fly the kingdom, as the discontented barons took up arms against his great influence and that of other foreign favorites introduced into England by the king. After an absence of two years he came back, under the protection of King Henry; but he was not suffered to land by the barons until he had sworn to observe the ordinances of Oxford. Nevertheless, not long after his arrival, the contest again broke out, and we find him holding one of the chief commands in the royal army. In conjunction with the prince he assaulted the town of Northampton, a stronghold of the barons, and put the whole baronial force to rout. But the rebels soon afterwards rallied, having been reinforced by the Londoners. The battle of Lewes followed, the royal army was defeated, and the king and the prince became prisoners. But William de Valence, who then bore the title of Earl of Pembroke, in company with the Earl of Warren and others, escaped by flight, first to Pevensey and thence to France. His estates were seized by the victorious rebels, and his wife, then residing at Windsor Castle, was ordered to retire immediately into some religious house. Later followed the battle of Evesham, the rebellious barons were dispersed, with great loss, and the power of the king reestablished. Immediately after the battle the possessions of William de Valence and others who had stood firm to the king, were restored, and, in addition, they were rewarded by large grants of lands which had formerly belonged to the rebellious barons.

During the reign of Edward I., in 1289, William de Valence and Joane his wife attempted to obtain the inheritance of Dionysia* (*Joane's niece*) by declaring her illegitimate.

---

* See " The Family of William de Lusignan (de Valence)," page 80.

In their petition to Parliament they set forth, "that, whereas, upon the death of William de Monchensi (*brother to the said Joane*), they had obtained a bull from the Pope directed to the Archbishop of Canterbury, touching the inheritance of the lands of the said William de Monchensi, thereby desiring that the king would please to commit the tuition of Dionysia, the daughter of the said William, unto some persons who might appear before the said archbishop, and such other judges as were named in the bull." But it was answered, " that the admission of the bull would tend to the diminution of the king's authority and power, by reason that such cases of hereditary succession ought not to be determined, but in his own courts. Wherefore, insomuch, as it did appear, that the object of the Earl was to invalidate the sentence of the Bishop of Worcester, which had declared the said Dionysia to be legitimate, and his design to make her a bastard, in order that he might enjoy her estate, his lordship and his lady were prohibited to prosecute their appeal any further." (*Burke.*)

His lordship was slain in 1296 while engaged in the wars of France. His remains were conveyed to England and interred in Westminster Abbey. By Joane, his wife, three sons and four daughters were born. Aymer, the only son living at the time of his death, succeeded as the Earl of Pembroke.

XXIV.

THE LUCYS OF CHARLECOTE, WARWICKSHIRE.

THURSTANE DE BASTENBURGH.

HUGH DE MONTFORT,
Invaded England with William the Conqueror.

HUGH DE MONTFORT.

ROBERT,	HUGH,	ALICE = GILBERT DE GAUNT,
Commander of the	While on a Crusade,	Grandson of
Army of William	d. sine prole.	Baldwin V.,
Rufus. d. sine prole.		Count of Flanders.

HUGH DE MONTFORT,= ADELINE,
Called daughter of Robert,
"*Hugh the Fourth.*" Earl of Millent.

ROBERT DE MONT-	THURSTANE DE MONT-	ADELINE,	(*Daughter*),
FORT.	FORT,	wife of Wil-	wife of Richard,
d. sine prole.	of Beldesert, suc-	liam de Bri-	son of the Earl
	ceeded his brother.	tollo.	of Gloucester.

HENRY DE MONTFORT, THURSTANE DE CHARLECOTE.
Succeeded his father.

SIR WALTER DE CHARLECOTE.

a

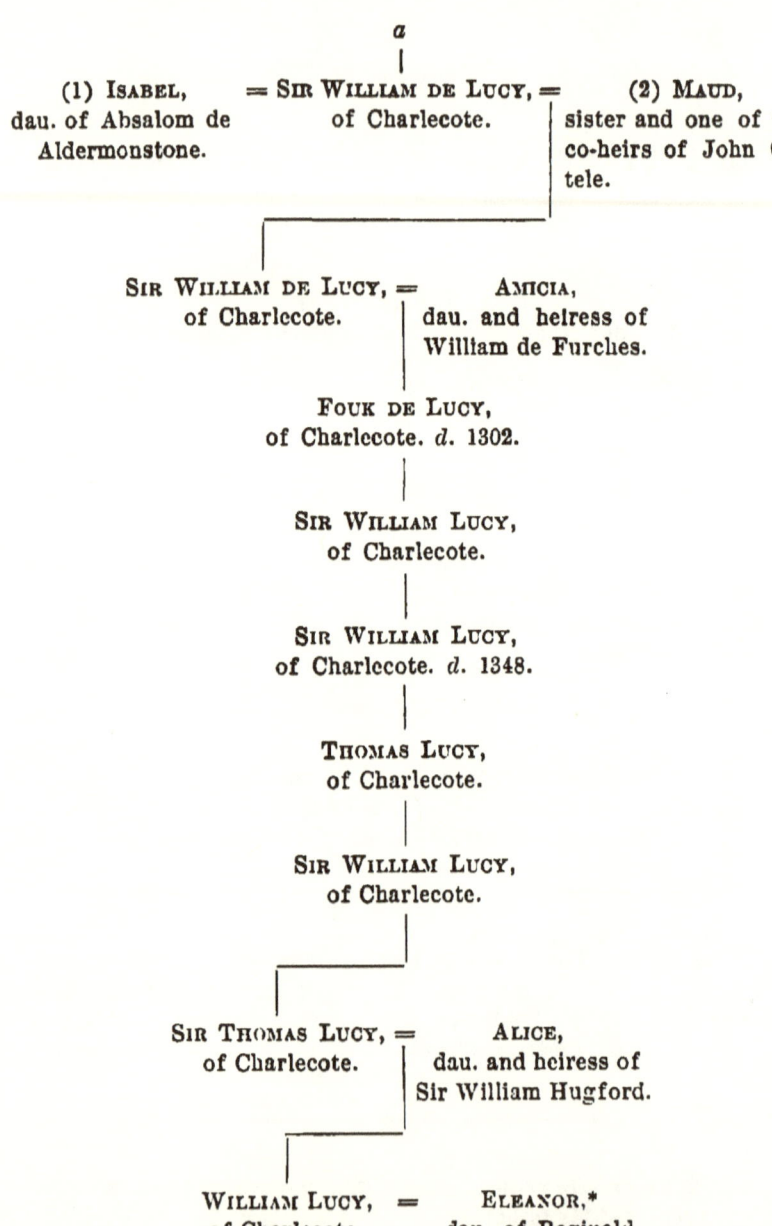

a

(1) ISABEL,   = SIR WILLIAM DE LUCY, =   (2) MAUD,
dau. of Absalom de   of Charlecote.   sister and one of the
Aldermonstone.   co-heirs of John Co-
                                                tele.

SIR WILLIAM DE LUCY, =   AMICIA,
of Charlecote.   dau. and heiress of
                      William de Furches.

FOUK DE LUCY,
of Charlecote. *d.* 1302.

SIR WILLIAM LUCY,
of Charlecote.

SIR WILLIAM LUCY,
of Charlecote. *d.* 1348.

THOMAS LUCY,
of Charlecote.

SIR WILLIAM LUCY,
of Charlecote.

SIR THOMAS LUCY, =   ALICE,
of Charlecote.   dau. and heiress of
                      Sir William Hugford.

WILLIAM LUCY,   =   ELEANOR,*
of Charlecote.   dau. of Reginald,
                      Lord Grey de Ruthvn.

---

* See " XIV. Lady Eleanor de Grey," page 66.

I. **HUGH DE MONTFORT**, commonly called "*Hugh with a Beard*," was a son of THURSTANE DE BASTENBURGH. This Hugh accompanied William of Normandy into England, and, not only at the battle of Hastings, but throughout the invasion and conquest which followed, rendered most eminent military service. For his services he seems to have been amply rewarded, for, at the time of the "general survey," he was possessed of twenty-eight lordships in Kent, with a large portion of Romney Marsh, sixteen in Essex, fifty-one in Suffolk, and nineteen in Norfolk. This gallant soldier eventually lost his life in a duel with Walcheline de Ferrers, and was succeeded by his son.

II. **HUGH DE MONTFORT**, who had issue by his first wife : —

> ROBERT, commander of the army of King William (*Rufus*), but, favoring the cause of Robert (*Curthose*), in opposition to Henry I., he was impeached for disloyalty. Conscious of his guilt, he started on a pilgrimage to Jerusalem, leaving all his possessions to the king. He died *sine prole*.
>
> HUGH, who also died *sine prole* while on a pilgrimage to Jerusalem.
>
> ALICE (*by his second wife*).

III. **ALICE DE MONTFORT**, the daughter by the second wife, was married to GILBERT DE GAUNT, a grandson of BALDWIN V., Count of Flanders, and had issue.

IV. **HUGH DE MONTFORT**, who, having assumed the surname of his mother's family, inherited all the possessions of his grandfather, and was commonly known as "*Hugh the Fourth*." This HUGH, having married ADELINE, a daughter of ROBERT, Earl of Millent, joined with Waleran, her brother, and all those who endeavored to advance the cause

of William, son of Robert-Curthose, against King Henry I.
in 1124. While in Normandy for this purpose, he and the
said Waleran were made prisoners and confined as such for
fourteen years. The time of his death is unknown, but he
left issue : —

> ROBERT, who fought and vanquished Henry de Essex, the king's
> standard bearer, having first charged him with cowardice, in
> fleeing from his colors (1163). He does not appear to have
> had any issue, for he was succeeded at his decease by his
> brother.
> THURSTANE, who succeeded his brother.
> ADELINE, who was married to William de Britolio.
> (*Daughter*), who was married to Richard, son of the Earl of
> Gloucester.

V. THURSTANE DE MONTFORT, who succeeded his
brother, Robert, "was enfeoffed of several lordships by
Henry de Newburgh, the first Earl of Warwick." At the
chief seat of his family in Warwickshire he erected a castle
of great strength, which he called "Beldesert." He was
succeeded by his eldest son.

> HENRY DE MONTFORT (*eldest son and successor*).
> THURSTANE DE CHARLECOTE.

VI. THURSTANE DE CHARLECOTE, a younger son of
Thurstane de Montfort, of Beldesert, in the County of Warwick, lived in the time of Richard I., and was father of —

VII. SIR WALTER DE CHARLECOTE, upon whom
Henry de Montfort conferred the village of Charlecote.
Richard I. confirmed the grant, and added many immunities

NOTE. "The Montforts," see Burke's "Extinct and Dormant Peerage."
"The Lucys of Charlecote" may be found in Burke's "History of the
Commoners."

and privileges, all of which were ratified by King John in the fifth year of that monarch's reign (1203). He left a son.

VIII. **SIR WILLIAM DE LUCY,** the first of the Charlecotes who bore that surname. Sir William Dugdale surmises that he took the surname of *De Lucy*, because his mother might have been the heir of some branch of the great baronial family of that name, which had derived its designation from a place in Normandy. Of this house was Henry de Lucy, so distinguished during the conflict between King Stephen and the Empress Maud, and who afterwards, during the reign of Henry II., was Justiciary of England; and who, at one time, during the temporary absence of the king beyond the sea, was lieutenant of the kingdom. During the reign of King John, Sir William de Lucy took up arms with the barons against the king, and in consequence, his estates were seized by the crown. Eventually he returned to his allegiance, and, in the first year of the reign of Henry III. (1216), a full restoration of all his possessions was made to him. In the twentieth year of the reign of the same monarch (1235), Sir William was placed in possession of the Castle of Kenilworth, and was given the custody of the counties of Warwick and Leicester. He married, first, Isabel, a daughter of Absalom de Aldermonstone, and, second, MAUD, sister and one of the co-heirs of John Cotele. He founded the monastery of Thelesford, and, dying about 1247, was succeeded by a son of his second wife.

IX. **SIR WILLIAM DE LUCY,** Knight of Charlecote, who wedded AMICIA, daughter and heiress of WILLIAM DE FURCHES, and heiress also of William Fitz-Warine, by whom he had a son and heir.

X. **FOUK DE LUCY,** who was in the immediate retinue of the celebrated Peter de Montfort, and who, after the battle of Lewes (*reign of Henry III.*), was constituted one of the nine governors of the kingdom.

"De Lucy acquired so much reputation by his gallantry in the Barons' War, that, being indebted to one Elyas de Blund, a Jew of London, in a large amount, he obtained a special mandate, dated 49 Henry III. (1264), and directed to the commissioners in whose hands the estates of the Jews then seized upon were entrusted, to deliver up to him all his bonds, and to cancel the debt. Subsequently, however, the royal cause having attained the ascendancy by the victorious arms of Prince Edward, De Lucy and his associates were glad to compromise for their estates under the *Dictum de Kenilworth.*" (*Burke's History of the Commoners.*)

"This Fouk was a special lover of good horses, as it would seem, for in the 11th of Edward I. he gave forty marks to two Londoners that were merchants of horses for a black charger, about which time a fat ox was sold for sixteen shillings." (*Sir William Dugdale.*)

He died in the thirty-first year of the reign of Edward I. (1302), and was succeeded by his son.

XI. **SIR WILLIAM LUCY,** of Charlecote, a person of celebrity in his generation. He was a representative in several Parliaments for the County of Warwick, and was succeeded by his son.

XII. **SIR WILLIAM LUCY,** of Charlecote. This Sir William, in the nineteenth year of the reign of Edward III. (1345), was summoned to attend the king into France, but, being engaged in raising and equipping one hundred and sixty archers from Warwickshire for the king's service, "his attendance was dispensed with, and he was thereby deprived of sharing in the glory of Cressy. He died in 1348, and was succeeded by his son."

XIII. **THOMAS LUCY,** of Charlecote, "who was succeeded at his decease by his son."

XIV. **SIR WILLIAM LUCY,** of Charlecote, "who, being a knight, was retained in the fifth year of the reign of Richard II. (1381), to serve John of Gaunt, Duke of Lancaster and King of Castile, for life, with one esquire, in times of war and peace." In the first year of the reign of Henry IV. (1399) he represented the County of Warwick in Parliament.

XV. **SIR THOMAS LUCY,** of Charlecote, his son and successor, was also in the retinue of John of Gaunt. In 1405 he was a member of Parliament for Warwickshire, and in the year following was Sheriff of the counties of Warwick and Leicester. He married ALICE, daughter and, eventually, heiress of SIR WILLIAM HUGFORD, and acquired through that lady estates in the counties of Bedford and Salop. He died July 28, 1415 (3 *Henry V.*),* leaving, by the said Alice, a son and successor.

XVI. **WILLIAM LUCY,†** of Charlecote, married LADY ELEANOR, daughter of REGINALD, LORD GREY DE RUTHYN.

---

* Eight weeks after the decease of Sir Thomas Lucy, his widow, Alice, married Richard Archer, of Tamworth.

† See "XIV. Lady Eleanor de Grey," page 66.

XXV.

THE BEAUCHAMPS,

ANCESTORS OF LADY ELIZABETH BEAUCHAMP, WIFE OF THOMAS DE
ASTLEY, THIRD LORD ASTLEY, AND OF BARBARA LUCY, WIFE OF
RICHARD TRACY OF STANWAY.

I. **HUGH DE BEAUCHAMP,** the companion in arms of
the victorious William of Normandy, was the recipient of
many favors and grants from that monarch. He possessed
large estates in Hertford, Buckingham, and Bedford shires.
This Hugh had issue, and his third son,—

II. **WALTER DE BEAUCHAMP,** of Elmley Castle, in
the County of Gloucester, having married EMELINE, daughter and heiress of URSO DE ABITOT, Constable of the Castle
of Worcester, and hereditary Sheriff of Worcestershire
(*who was brother of Robert le Despenser, steward to the
Conqueror*), was invested with that sheriffalty by King
Henry I., and obtained a grant from the same monarch (*to
whom he was steward*) of all the lands belonging to Roger
de Worcester, with a confirmation of certain lands given to
him by ADELISE, widow of his father-in-law, the said URSO.
Walter de Beauchamp was succeeded, as well in his estates
as in the royal stewardship, by his son,—

III. **WILLIAM DE BEAUCHAMP.** This nobleman,
having aided the Empress Maud in her endeavors to gain
the English throne, was deprived of all his honors and dis-
possessed of his estates by King Stephen. But, when
Henry II. (*son of the Empress Maud*) succeeded to the
throne (1153), not only were all his previous honors

and estates restored to him, but, besides the sheriffalty of Worcestershire, which he enjoyed by inheritance, he was made Sheriff of Warwickshire, Sheriff of Gloucestershire, and Sheriff of Herefordshire. Upon the levy of the assessment towards the marriage portion of one of King Henry's daughters, this feudal lord certified his knight's fees to amount to fifteen. He married MAUD, daughter of WILLIAM, LORD BRAOSE, of Gower, and was succeeded at his death by his son,—

IV. **WILLIAM DE BEAUCHAMP,** who married JOANE, a daughter of SIR THOMAS WALERIE, died before 1211 (13 *John*), leaving a son, WALTER, a minor, whose wardship and marriage Roger de Mortimer and Isabel, his wife, obtained for 3000 marks.

V. **WALTER DE BEAUCHAMP.** This feudal lord was appointed governor of Hanley Castle, in the County of Worcester, in 1215 (17 *John*), and was entrusted with the custody of the same shire in that turbulent year. But, proving faithless to the king, and joining the insurrectionery barons, all his lands were seized by the crown and himself excommunicated, a course of proceeding which extorted immediate submission, for we find him very soon afterwards making his peace with the king, and soliciting absolution from Gualo, the legate. Absolution he seems to have obtained, for, upon giving security to Henry III., who had just then succeeded to the throne (1216), he had restitution of his castle at Worcester, with his hereditary sheriffalty. He married BERTHA, daughter of WILLIAM, LORD BRAOSE, by whom he had two sons, WALCHELINE and JAMES. He died in 1235, and was succeeded by his elder son.

VI. **WALCHELINE DE BEAUCHAMP** married JOANE, daughter of ROGER, LORD MORTIMER, and, dying in the same year as his father (1235), was succeeded by an only son,—

VII. **WILLIAM DE BEAUCHAMP**, the feudal Lord of Elmley. This nobleman distinguished himself by the efficient military service which he rendered to the crown during the reign of Henry III. In 1252 he was with the king in Gascogne; in 1254 he marched against the Scots under the banner of the Earl of Gloucester; later he was summoned, with other illustrious persons, to meet the king at Chester on the first day of Saint Peter, "well fitted with horse and arms," to oppose the incursions of Leweline, Prince of Wales. Many other similar summonses were, from time to time, received by his lordship, the highest proof at that period of power, prowess, and loyalty.

Lord Beauchamp married ISABEL, daughter of WILLIAM MAUDUIT, of Hanslape, in the County of Berks, and sister and heiress of William Mauduit, Earl of Warwick. He died in 1268, and was succeeded by his eldest son,—

VIII. **WILLIAM DE BEAUCHAMP.** This nobleman inherited from his father the feudal barony of Elmley, and from his mother the Earldom of Warwick (*originally possessed by the Newburgs*), and the barony of Hanslape (*which had belonged to the Mauduits*). In the Welsh and Scottish wars, waged during the reign of Edward I., he rendered most efficient service to the king and distinguished himself as a military leader.

" In the 23d year of which reign (*Edward I.*), being in Wales with the king, he performed a notable exploit; namely, hearing that a great body of the Welsh were got together in a plain, betwixt two woods, and to secure themselves, had fastened their pikes to the ground, slopping towards their assailants, he marched thither with a choice company of cross-bow-men and archers, and in the night time, encompassing them about, put betwixt every two horsemen, one cross-bow-man, which cross-bow-man, killing many of them that held the pikes, the horse charged in suddenly, and made a great slaughter. This was done near Montgomery." (*Dugdale*.)

His lordship married MAUD, widow of Girard de Furnival, and one of the four daughters and co-heiresses of RICHARD FITZ-JOHN, son of JOHN FITZ-GEFFERY, Chief Justice of Ireland, by whom he had issue. He was succeeded by his eldest son,—

IX. **GUY DE BEAUCHAMP,** *second* Earl of Warwick, so called in memory of his celebrated predecessor, — "the Saxon Guy." Like his father, he acquired high military renown. For the distinguished part which he took at the battle of Falkirk, he was rewarded with extensive grants of land in Scotland. He also distinguished himself at the siege of Cærlaverock, and upon several occasions in expeditions beyond the sea. In 1310 (*Edward II.*) he was a member of the commission appointed by Parliament to draw up regulations for "the well governing of the kingdom and the king's household," in consequence of the corrupt influence exercised at that period in the affairs of the realm by Piers Gaveston, through the unbounded partiality of the king. Upon the surrender of Scarborough Castle, in 1312, Gaveston fell into the hands of his enemies, and, after a summary trial, the Earl caused him to be beheaded at Blacklow Hill, near Warwick.* For this atrocious proceeding the Earl and all others concerned were eventually pardoned by the king.

---

* The Earl of Warwick's hostility to Gaveston is said to have been much increased by learning that the favorite had nicknamed him " *The Black Dog of Ardenne.*"

His lordship married ALICE, widow of Thomas de Laybourne, and a daughter of RALPH DE TONI of Flamsted, in the County of Hertford, and by her had issue. He died at Warwick Castle August 12, 1315. It is supposed that he was poisoned by the partisans of Gaveston.

His children were : —

> THOMAS, his heir and successor.
> JOHN, who was Captain of Calais, Admiral of the Fleet, Standard Bearer at Cressy, and one of the original Knights of the Garter; he was also summoned to Parliament as a baron.
> MAUD, wife of Geoffrey, Lord Say.
> EMMA, wife of Rowland Odingsels.
> ISABEL, wife of John Clinton.
> ELIZABETH,* wife of Thomas, Lord Astley.
> LUCIA, wife of Robert de Napton.

---

* See " VII. Thomas de Astley, third Lord Astley," pages 78, 79.

XXVI.

THE NORMAN DUKES.

DESCENT OF EMMA OF NORMANDY AND WILLIAM THE CONQUEROR.

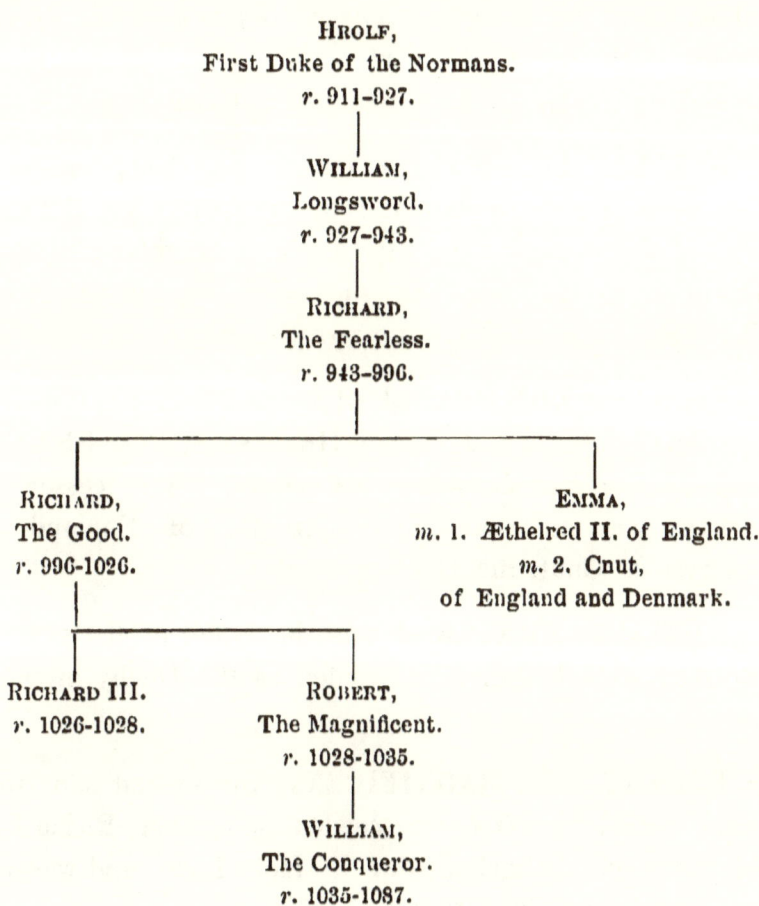

HROLF,
First Duke of the Normans.
r. 911–927.

WILLIAM,
Longsword.
r. 927–943.

RICHARD,
The Fearless.
r. 943–996.

RICHARD,
The Good.
r. 996–1026.

EMMA,
m. 1. Æthelred II. of England.
m. 2. Cnut,
of England and Denmark.

RICHARD III.
r. 1026–1028.

ROBERT,
The Magnificent.
r. 1028–1035.

WILLIAM,
The Conqueror.
r. 1035–1087.

HROLF, sometimes *Rollo,* or *Raoul,* was a Norwegian pirate, and succeeded in wresting the land on both sides of the mouth of the Seine from the French king, Charles the Simple. By the treaty in which France purchased peace, the coast about the mouth of the Seine was ceded to HROLF, and he became a vassal to the French king for the territory which took the name of *"The Northman's Land,"* or Normandy. Hrolf was also baptized in the Christian faith, and was given Gesla, the king's daughter, in marriage.

WILLIAM-LONGSWORD, his son and heir, was by his first wife, POPPA, a daughter of the COUNT DE BAYEAUX. This William, took for a wife Adela, a daughter of Hubert, Count de Seulis. He was succeeded by his eldest son, RICHARD, known as RICHARD THE FEARLESS.

RICHARD THE FEARLESS married GUNORA, sometimes written *Gunred,* a daughter of HERBASTUS, a Danish knight, and by her had RICHARD THE GOOD, his successor, and EMMA, who married ÆTHELRED II., of England, and afterwards Cnut, the Dane.

RICHARD THE GOOD was the father of RICHARD and ROBERT, each of whom succeeded to the Duchy in succession.

ROBERT THE MAGNIFICENT, the second son, sometimes called *"le diable,"* succeeded his brother, Richard III. He went on a pilgrimage to the Holy Land, and was poisoned at Nicæa, in Bithynia, 1035.

WILLIAM, Duke of Normandy, surnamed *"The Conqueror,"* from his triumph over Harold at Hastings, October 14, 1066, was crowned King of England by Aldred, Archbishop of York, at Westminster Abbey, on the 25th of

December of the same year. He was the illegitimate son of ROBERT THE MAGNIFICENT, by ARLOTTA, the daughter of a tanner of Falaise, and was born in 1025. His father, Duke Robert, had no legitimate children, and, upon his departure to the Holy Land, persuaded the barons to swear allegiance to young William as his heir. In 1053 William married MATILDA, sometimes called MAUD, a daughter of BALDWIN V., Count of Flanders,*

It has been computed that during the invasion and reign of William I. one third of the old Saxon population of England was swept from the land. Terrible as are the acts of cruelty and oppression with which William's memory is associated, it would be unjust to let them blind us to the high qualities which he displayed as a soldier, a sovereign, and as an ordainer of English institutions. His dominion and his dynasty he was resolved to establish firmly in England, and neither fear nor mercy ever made him pause in employing the most efficacious means to bring about this end. He died September 9, 1087, at Hermentrude, a suburb of Rouen, and was interred in the Church of St. Stephen at Caen.

By his wife, Matilda, four sons and six daughters were born : —

ROBERT (*Courthose*), succeeded his father as Duke of Normandy, but sold the duchy to his brother William, and joined the Crusaders. Issue extinct.

RICHARD, died *sine prole*.

WILLIAM (*Rufus*), succeeded his father as King of England. Reigned as William II., 1087-1100.

NOTE. Hugh, surnamed "Lupus," the nephew of William the Conqueror, and the second Earl of Chester, in England, was a grandson of this Arlotta of Falaise. See "The Norman Descent of Sir William de Traci," page 31, and foot note, page 29.

* See "Count Baldwin V.," page 49.

HENRY, usurped the throne upon the death of his brother, William. Reigned as Henry I., 1100-1135; married, Matilda, daughter of Malcolm III., King of Scotland.

CICELY, Lady Abbess at Caen.

CONSTANTIA, married to Alan Forgaunt, Earl of Brittany.

ALICE, died unmarried.

ADELA, married to Stephen, Count of Blois. Her son, Stephen, succeeded his uncle, Henry I., as King of England.

AGATHA, died unmarried.

GUNDRED,* married to William de Warrenne,† Earl of Warrenne, in Normandy, and of Surrey, in England.

---

* The birth of the Princess Gundred is disputed by some authorities, and she has been called " *The Mysterious Gundred.*" The Earl of Surrey, however, states that his wife was the daughter of the Queen Matilda.

† See " I. William de Warrenne," page 59.